THE RIO KID
RIDES AGAIN

	DATE DUE	
AL LR		
BC		
GC		
EW		

GAYLORD #3523PI Printed in USA

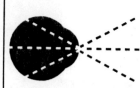 This Large Print Book carries the
Seal of Approval of N.A.V.H.

THE RIO KID
RIDES AGAIN

TOM CURRY

WHEELER PUBLISHING
A part of Gale, Cengage Learning

GALE
CENGAGE Learning

Detroit • New York • San Francisco • New Haven, Conn • Waterville, Maine • London

GALE
CENGAGE Learning

Copyright © 1940 by Tom Curry.
Copyright © renewed 1968 by Tom Curry.
A Rio Kid Western.
Wheeler Publishing, a part of Gale, Cengage Learning.

LIBRARY OF CONGRESS CATALOGING-IN-PUBLICATION DATA

Curry, Tom, 1900–
   The Rio Kid rides again / by Tom Curry.
     p. cm. — (A Rio Kid western) (Wheeler Publishing large
  print western)
   ISBN-13: 978-1-59722-806-0 (pbk. : alk. paper)
   ISBN-10: 1-59722-806-0 (pbk. : alk. paper) 1. Large type
books. I. Title.
PS3505.U9725R56 2008
813'.52—dc22   2008017938

Published in 2008 by arrangement with Golden West Literary Agency.

Printed in the United States of America
1 2 3 4 5 6 7 12 11 10 09 08

THE RIO KID
RIDES AGAIN

CHAPTER I
WAR FOR WAR

Daniel Worrell started awake, his big hand reaching for the heavy rifle that was never far from him night or day. The Texas Border country was so upset by the constantly increasing depredations of stock thieves that Worrell was doubly alert. He was determined to protect his small spread a few miles north of the Rio Grande.

He had a special motive in this ambition to make a home and a good living. Pioneers are hard to scare, and Worrell came of that hardy stock which braved Indian raids and difficult times.

Even as he leaped up and cocked the rifle, he caught the ugly gurgling of a man whose throat was filled with choking blood. But this quickly ceased. Death had come in the night.

"That was Miguel," he growled.

He sprang to the little window slit, made like a fort's, looking toward the barn where his Mexican cowboys slept. He started to cry out to his friends, but checked himself at the last moment. That would only give away his position.

A half moon cast a bright light over the clearing in the chaparral. Near the square barn he saw a band of about twenty riders. One struck a match to light a cigarette. Worrell, rifle rising to firing position, could make out the man's fierce, sharp, red face, the thin, long nose. The shoulder-length carrot-colored hair hanging from under his Stetson matched his beard.

"Hustle, Gonzales," ordered the redhead, with a leader's commanding tone. "Go take care of yore man in the cabin. He's likely to bother us."

A slim vaquero in dark velvet, metal conchas of his high-peaked sombrero glinting in the moonlight, showed his white teeth as he waved a foot-long bowie knife.

"*Si*, Senor Vance. I have bone to peek weeth Worrell. Las' mont' he keel one of my best bravos who was takin' off some cows from here."

"Xavier Gonzales!" Worrell grunted.

He remembered the incident. He had come on three Mexican stock thieves brazenly driving fifty head of his steers toward the Rio Grande. When he tried to stop them they had opened fire and he killed one, wounded a second and run off the third. This victory had heartened Worrell. Besides, it wasn't in his blood to quit without a struggle.

"Don't leave no witnesses," he heard Vance say. "Touch a match to the thatch roof."

Wide lips set, Dan Worrell took aim and squeezed his rifle trigger. But just as he shot, Gonzales shifted, heading toward the shack. The Mexican bravo certainly felt the slug. It nipped his ribs, but only cut him and plugged into one of the men following. The latter threw up both arms, emitted a shrill screech and fell from his bucking mustang.

Immediately the whole gang dug in their spurs and split up, madly hunting cover. Gonzales, stung by the wound, blood spurting from his lacerated flesh, jerked his bronc around into the dense shadows on the other side of the barn. Sorreltop Vance was already on his way. The Mexicans bumped one another in their eagerness to escape.

Worrell fired two more shots. He hit a man each time, but he was too wary a fighter to remain in the shack. He could not hold off such a gang for long. They would surround the cabin and have him. The ranch

9

was far from any neighbors and both of his helpers were dead. He could see the dark, still bodies of the victims lying on the dusty earth near the open barn door. Gonzales must have sent in some scouts on foot and caught them before they could get organized to fight.

Worrell paused only to fill his pockets with cartridges and buckle on his wide belt with its holstered Frontier Model Colt .45 revolver. He ran to the door at the other end of his home and out into the yard.

A fusillade banged back. Bullets thudded into the adobe brick wall, tore through the window. Down low he scudded for the bush, a tall, stalwart figure bent at the waist. He had missed the Civil War by a year or two, being too young to take part in the terrible fraternal struggle. But now he was a fully grown man.

His shrewdness in leaving the cabin was quickly justified. Already he could hear them shoving through the brush from both flanks, meaning to surround the clearing. He hit the chaparral. A couple of bullets zipped in the dry leaves nearby, revealing that those on the other side, who were not busy riding, had glimpsed him as he ran.

Something bit at his sleeve and a twinge of pain ran up his left arm. But it was only a crease that did not stop him from hiding in the chaparral, the stunted jungle which covered so much of this land. He hit out for the winding trail through the thorned bush. Crouching in the dense shadow cast by a mesquite clump, he laid his rifle on the earth. He heard a rider pushing up. A minute later appeared a dark-faced Mexican bravo, eyes gleaming, pistol in right hand, guiding his hairy black mustang expertly with his left.

Worrell had his six-shooter drawn. He straightened his powerful legs, coming erect. It was life or death, and this was his single chance.

He fired pointblank as the bravo hurriedly took aim. The Mexican's gun exploded, but the bullet kicked up dust between Worrell's bare feet. He had not had time to pull on his boots or get his hat. The moment he fired, his left hand snatched at the bronc's reins and got them. The beast fought madly at the flashes of the guns and the reports which echoed sharply in the night.

Worrell jerked the horse around. The motion threw off the bravo who would kill no more victims in Texas. Keeping tight hold of the mustang's bridle rein, he stooped and grabbed up his rifle. Then he mounted, shoving his bare feet into the narrow, tapaderos-protected stirrups and starting away swiftly. Some were coming after him, and the shots had attracted the others farther away.

Knowing the surrounding land like a familiar book, Dan Worrell flashed through the winding trails, leaving behind him the belongings for which he had worked so hard the past two years. A cold rage ate at his heart. His motive in setting up that spread had been an honest one. She lived in Smithville, twenty miles east of the ranch.

"Damn them!" he growled, eyes glowing ferociously, as he glanced back over his wide shoulder.

The black was a fast one. The gang could not follow him long, and did not try too hard. It was Worrell's stock they were after and they quickly took it, adding to a large herd being driven for the ford across the Rio Grande.

In Cuba, the patriots had been fighting Spain for their liberty since just after the American Civil War. Steers fetched eighteen dollars a head in Monterey, army beef which Mexicans contracted to deliver. So no Texan's stock was safe for hundreds of miles around, up and down the river and inland as well. The isolated individuals sweated blood, fought and died against the marauding bands of stock thieves. Small bands were of no avail against the growing hordes of raiders. Red tape tied the hands of the small, scattered army posts.

To the northwest, Worrell, stopping the lathered mustang when he had shaken off his pursuers, saw a red glow in the sky.

"That must be McCall's," he grunted aloud.

It was the ranch of Worrell's nearest neighbor. A couple of women and some children had been there, besides Tim Mc-Call and his brother Ed. No doubt the same gang which had hit him had raided the McCalls'.

He began working along a trail north of his spread. By the time he came up above his home, he could see the mounting red flames over his clearing.

"Damn them!" he growled again.

Nothing remained but revenge. Those who dared fight back against the stock thieves paid with their lives and destruction of their property. Dan Worrell had killed two bravos and wounded several more, among them Xavier Gonzales, one of the best-known of the thieves from General Juan Flores' Las Cuevas Ranch in Mexico.

It was dawn when, after his hard ride, Dan Worrell pulled into the little Texas town of

Smithville. Set along a tributary creek of the Rio Grande, in the chaparral country north of the Border, Smithville had mostly a Mexican and half-breed population. But there was a small number of Anglo-American Texans in the town. Built in Southwest style, around a cleared plaza, its stores all had wooden sun-awnings. Most of the houses were of adobe brick, the best ones whitewashed, the older ones made of boards, with thatched roofs.

Despite the earliness of the hour, the town was in an uproar, and Worrell, disheveled from his experiences, wondered what was wrong. Mexicans were crowded in a knot around a good-size adobe home. Horses stood saddled and ready. Worrell headed for the large, square building of thick logs, over which a sign said:

GEORGE PURCELL
GROCERIES, FEED AND HARDWARE

He swung from the mustang, stepped up on the veranda of the general store. A young woman stood there, staring at the crowd across the way. She turned. Recognizing Worrell, her large blue eyes lighted with surprised joy. She was slim in the white dress she had hastily slipped on, and her dark hair was piled on her trim head. She was young and pretty and she put up red lips for Worrell to kiss.

"Daniel, I'm so glad you're here! But — what's wrong?"

Conchita Purcell, the storeowner's only child, was the reason for Daniel Worrell's earnest purpose in life. For her he had been getting ready the spread which through wanton criminality had been destroyed in a few minutes.

The smile left Conchita's face. Half Irish and half Spanish, her emotions were quick to respond. She took in Worrell's set, scratched face, the blood on his arm, the gleam of his eyes.

"You're all right?" she gasped, clinging to him.

"Sure, sure. But, damn them! Gonzales burned my ranch and run off all my stock, Conchita. I'll get 'em for it."

"No, you be careful." She hugged him. "I won't let you go, dear one. I'm afraid. Why, it's not safe, even here in town!"

"What's wrong?"

"Another murder, this time Rafael Ortez. He was my mother's first cousin. Sheriff Carr is over there now. So is Dad."

She gave Dan a pair of boots to put on, and he strolled over and pushed through

15

the excited Mexicans. He went into the house, hearing the wailing of Ortez' wife.

In the candle-lit main room up front were several men. Among them was the short, broad George Purcell, Conchita's widower father, a man with brown hair and blue eyes, which his daughter had inherited. His big mouth and broad Irish face were usually good-humored. Now they were grim with the baffled anger he felt at the mysterious murder.

Sheriff Dave Carr, in charge of the investigation, was tall and loose-jointed, a powerful fellow with a slow way of moving. He wore blue pants tucked into high black-leather riding boots, long spurred. A leather vest dangled open to his bony hips, which were girded with a cartridge belt heavy with brass shells for the two browned-steel Colts riding his holsters. He was frowning as he stared down at the corpse on the mat, a Mexican who had been stabbed to the heart in his sleep. Rafael Ortez had died quickly without even crying out, his hysterical wife said.

"Now what the hell!" snapped Sheriff Dave Carr.

Worrell could look over George Purcell's short figure and see what the sheriff held in one bronzed, calloused hand. It was a chunk of cured cowhide, blackened by the sun. About six inches across at the top, it was carved in the rough shape of a heart.

"The Black Heart!" George Purcell cried.

"Yeah. Funny, this is the fourth such murder in this county in the past month," Carr said. "And I found one of these beside every corpse!"

"The world's shore gone to hell and all the way," Purcell complained. "Stock thieves hittin' everywhere in southeast Texas. Nobody safe in his bed at night any more. We got to reach the bottom of this Black Heart business, Sheriff. It's some kind of secret society, I'll bet, that means to wipe us all out."

"Yuh may be right, George," Sheriff Carr agreed. "It's up to the law to git to the bottom of this. I'm workin' night and day till I catch up with these dirty murderers."

Dan Worrell rested through the warm day in a shack behind Purcell's store. He turned over the situation in his mind. The scattered Texans were fighting in the wrong way, he decided. They needed to be organized against the bandits. On the other hand, that meant leaving their stock and homes to the mercy of the enemy, and these pioneers would not want to do that.

The small army posts along the Rio had

17

too few men in them to venture against the hordes of the bold rustlers. The country was so vast it was almost impossible to catch up with them. And spies were swarming through the land, ever ready to warn the outlaws from over the Border.

Army red tape forbade crossing the Rio after them. Any small force that did so, a sheriff's posse or vigilante band, would immediately be wiped out by the hundreds of fighting bravos. Several sheriffs had died trying this.

That evening after dark, Worrell went to a saloon to talk with the angry, upset men of the community. On his way back to Purcell's later, humming a tune and thinking of Conchita, Dan passed the inky black mouth of a narrow alley. No one showed near at hand. He wasn't thinking of danger here.

He heard a slight swish behind him, and tried to draw his gun and whirl, ready to fight. Before he could get his weapon out of the holster, he was struck a blinding, terrible blow from the rear. Stunning blackness overcame him. His knees buckled and he folded up on the sidewalk. A burly figure seized him, dragged him into the alley.

Chapter II
Secret Canyon

Captain Robert Pryor, formerly of Custer's brigade in the Union Army, crooned to his wicked-eyed dun, Saber, as they shoved for the Rio.

"Said the big black charger
To the little white mare,
The sergeant claims yore feed bill
Really ain't fair —"

It was Saber's favorite tune and the black stripe along the dun's back rippled appreciation. He would run in answer to a few whistled bars of it when Pryor wanted him.

Pryor, known as the Rio Kid through Texas and the Frontier, where his exploits had made him a famous figure, swung in his leather.

"Those hombres ahead seem in a powerful hurry with that bunch of stock, Celestino," he remarked to the slim Mexican

19

youth coming behind.

"*Si*, General," Celestino Mireles replied.

Dark of eyes and hair, wearing a sombrero, Mireles looked with dog-like affection at his leader.

The Rio Kid was a figure to attract the glances of men and women. His blue eyes held a reckless, devil-may-care light, that revealed something of his unfailing courage and power. He carried two fine, browned-steel army Colts in black-leather holster belt, and under his clothing two more small guns.

Inured to peril, the Kid had felt it impossible to settle down after the excitement of serving as scout for General George A. Custer in the Civil War. Though he had been born on the Rio Grande, he had chosen to fight for the Union. But on returning home after the end of the awful conflict where brother slaughtered brother, he had found his home and people destroyed by invading criminals. Frontier guns had avenged the Texans. Then he had guided a group of persecuted Confederates up the cattle trail to Kansas. He had been a Frontier marshal, a buffalo hunter, and a scout.

Now, on a special mission which had to do with his friend and comrade, Celestino

Mireles, whom the Rio Kid had snatched from death, the two were riding for the Rio Grande.

His years as an army man had given the Kid a military bearing, an air of command that nothing could eradicate. He had a passion for neatness, and his gear was always kept in meticulous order. An army carbine rode under his booted leg, a belt of ammunition for it hanging from the horn of his expensive saddle.

Saber, his pet horse, was a fit riding mate for the Rio Kid. The dun had a black stripe along his spine, the "breed that never dies." He was not prepossessing in appearance, but he was a devil in a fight. He actually seemed to enjoy gunfire, for he would gallop toward it if not checked. His hide showed several bullet weals. The Rio Kid sported a number of such scars himself, notably one over his ribs which itched when danger threatened.

Now Celestino, the patrician Mexican with the aquiline nose and curved lips, pushed his horse closer to the Kid. They had come upon a fresh trail left by a number of driven animals. They had been following it only because the road led the way they wished to go and they were in a hurry.

"Perhaps, General," the Mexican youth

remarked, "zese hombres ahead would not weesh us to come too near!"

Pryor nodded. He reached in his blue-shirt pocket for the makin's, rolling himself a quirly as the saddle faintly creaked with the dun's motion.

"Maybe yuh're right, Celestino. Stock thieves would be in a hurry. But we can't let that delay us."

Word had come to Mireles that several of his cousins had been murdered in southeast Texas. The young man had followed the Rio Kid through thick and thin. Now that he wished to invade the district and avenge the crimes, Pryor had readily agreed to accompany him, and they had started for Smithville, Texas.

They were riding a dirt trail, through a scrub forest, which wound in and out with the contours of the land. Still thirty miles from their destination, they mounted a rise.

"There's dust ahead, Celestino," the Kid said.

The cloud hung thicker over the trail. Slow to settle, it meant they were treading on the heels of the unseen men before them. The Rio Kid was too wary a campaigner to shove up on hombres who might resent such an intrusion. Also, he was in a hurry, and the land was none too open for cross-

22

country riding.

The scarred flesh over his ribs twitched, and Saber grew restless, sniffing, though the wind was at their back. The Rio Kid slowed down at the next turn in the trail. A man in heavy leather, bandanna drawn up to his eyes, leaped into the path, his hands full of Colts.

"Hold it," said Pryor, jerking his reins as the startled dun shied and snorted.

He knew the ways of such folks. If the gang ahead were running stolen stock, they would have a rear guard hanging back to watch the trail for pursuers. He instantly concluded the gunny whose eyes blazed with fierce rage must be one of them. He sought to open a parley, but the man with the revolvers fired at once.

Pryor went out from under his Stetson as the bullet grazed his cheek and broke the strap holding it under his chin. The dun's lunge caused the second one to miss. The Kid's hand moved like a blurring brown flash to his army revolver.

The gunny bent over in a shooting crouch, swung his weapons on Pryor. He was taking no chances. Without doubt, the stock had been stolen, and a guilty conscience is a dangerous accompaniment to armed thieves.

The Rio Kid's Colt barked once. As he fired, from the corner of his left eye he caught a rapid, scintillating flash. His bullet took the horse thief in the right shoulder and smashed the bone. It would disable the man, merely put him out of commission. Pryor had not shot to kill but to protect himself.

As the hombre's revolvers flew from his relaxed hands, Pryor heard a dull thud. Mireles, seeking to save his friend, had let fly his razor-sharp bowie knife. It drove with full force into the gunny's breast, striking home to his heart. He fell lifeless to the trail.

"Yuh settled his hash, Celestino," the Kid growled, wiping blood off his cheek.

He turned Saber, who was sniffing at the fresh scent of gore and burnt powder. Bending far down, Pryor swept up his hat, tied a knot in the chin strap and replaced the Stetson.

"Si, General. He meant to keel," Mireles replied calmly.

He dismounted from his roan mustang. Placing one foot on the dead man's chest, he pulled out his favorite knife. He wiped it on the victim's shirt and slipped it back into its scabbard under his trouser leg.

"Perhaps," Celestino remarked, "eet would be best eef you tak' off zat badge,

24

General. Zey do not savvy."

"Dawggone, I reckon yuh're right. I've had it on so long, it got to be part of the scenery."

The Rio Kid, having been a marshal in Ellsworth, Kansas, had neglected to remove his badge of office. He unpinned the marshal's insignia and shied it off into the bushes.

"Zey come," warned Mireles, hand dropping to his gun.

The explosions had reverberated on the wind, carrying to those ahead. Shouts and shots sounded and half a dozen hard-faced riders came hell-for-leather back at them.

"Hey, Dinny!" one shouted, evidently addressing the deceased killer.

"No use tryin' to explain," whispered the Kid.

The oncoming gunmen had sighted them, and angry yells and bullets roared toward them. To avoid a hopeless encounter, there was nothing to do but ride for it and attempt to evade the covering fighting men of the stock thieves ahead.

Saber sought to run toward the attackers. But the Kid spoke soothingly to the dun. Kicking the rump of Mireles' roan, he started the Mexican ahead of him eastward through the bush.

Mireles was practically a centaur. Like the Kid, he had been able to ride before he could walk, and his blood made him a natural genius with horses.

"There they go!"

The furious gunnies, seeing their dead comrade in the trail, swerved to follow Pryor.

About an hour more of light remained before the sun would suddenly go down, plunging the bush into darkness. Bullets were zipping about them, clipping leaves, thudding into dirt. Suddenly Mireles gave a curse of pain. Blood ran from a slash in his arm.

"Ride on, pronto," ordered Pryor.

Anger raced in his veins, but no emotion could disturb the Kid's fighting abilities. He was too accustomed to danger to let his eye and steady nerves be upset by peril.

Mireles, knowing that his friend must not be disobeyed, spurted on ahead. The Rio Kid swung in his leather, began firing back at the wolfish desperadoes who came screeching and shooting at him through the chaparral.

He clipped a horse. Its rider crashed head-first into a thorn bush. Pryor's aim, extraordinarily accurate from the back of a speeding horse, worried the gunnies. They spread out, keeping a respectful distance. Yet they would not give up, but trailed like determined hounds after him. Blood-revenge for Dinny's death urged them on. They also feared the man ahead might be a spy for the law.

Celestino had ridden due east, disappearing behind a knoll. The Rio Kid wanted to give his wounded partner a chance to escape. He drew his pursuers at a south angle, led them on for half an hour through the rolling, timbered country. The sun was coming closer to the horizon behind him. It was difficult for him to shoot when he looked back, with the blinding light directly in his eyes.

Then he let the dun have his head, and Saber drew away from the pack of gunnies. They gave up at last. Swinging around, they cut for the beaten trail where their mates were driving the stolen stock.

Making sure they were no longer after him, Pryor turned north, expecting to locate Mireles. He came on the Mexican's track, which led east. But darkness caught him before he came up with the Mexican lad. He rode on, more slowly, under a rising moon. The shadows were inky, and Saber was lathered and tired from the race. The Kid decided he would pick up his friend in

27

the light of the next day. About to dismount and camp overnight, he saw far ahead a faint light.

His first thought was that it was a signal from Mireles. He was up on a plateaulike wooded rise, and the light was down below. Proceeding in the moonlight, he found the way blocked by a deep ravine in which he could glimpse the silver ribbon of a little stream.

He turned south along this precipitous *barranca*. For a mile he could find no possible way down, yet from the cut he could hear the bawling of many steers. Then he realized that the light he had seen came from the window of a house.

"Now who's runnin' a ranch in this God-forsaken hole?" he muttered.

CHAPTER III
DEN OF THIEVES

Bob Pryor came to a break in the canyon wall, a steep rock slide where water had eroded the red stone and made a dangerous but negotiable path into the split. It was too much for a horse with a rider on his back, so he dismounted. With Saber's reins in one hand, he started the descent. The dun, sure-footed as a mountain burro, slid along with his master. But small rocks were dislodged and tumbled down before him.

They descended on the west side of the little stream of water that meandered through the deep but narrow canyon. The noise of the steers echoed between the rock walls. The Kid paused to look at the great corrals, built of long poles and thorn bushes. How many steers they contained, he did not know. There were hundreds, at least. The entire box canyon had been closed off at the north end. The stream afforded plenty of water for the stock.

"Mighty slick place to hold cows," he mused, as he swung along a narrow path that led to the back of the house.

He left the dun loose to graze and rest in the widening mouth of the *barranca*. Saber would come at his whistle and would not let other men catch him if he could avoid it. Then, cautiously, meaning to make a survey before he walked into a possible outlaw hideout, Pryor crossed the brook by a stepping-stone. He silently approached the lighted side window.

The house had several rooms in it, but was hastily constructed of logs and loose rocks, with a thatched roof. The windows were narrow. A few were open to let in air, but the others, covered with greased paper, let in only the light.

Over the sounds made by the cattle in the corrals up the canyon, Pryor heard the hum of voices. He was startled and put off guard by the musical tones of a woman. This conjured up a picture of a cozy pioneer home. Maybe he had been wrong in believing he had run upon a rustler's den.

Carefully he raised his eyes to peep over the window ledge, and looked into a square front room. There were rough chairs made of boxes and log lengths about. On a big pine table stood a bottle of whiskey, a slab of beef, and a loaf of home-baked bread. The woman, pretty and youthful, sat at one end of the table, sewing on a leather gun-belt. She wore a flowered dress, a white apron, and her whole appearance was feminine and neat.

A handsome but depraved looking youth was alone in the room with her. They were talking about beef cattle, and the man remarked that eighteen dollars a head was enough to make them rich.

"Maybe so," the woman said, "but it'll take a lot to make me think I'm rich, Blue Duck."

"I reckon yuh're right, Belle," the Blue Duck said with a humorous wink, "after them duds yuh bought on yore last trip to Dallas."

"Is that any business of yours?" Belle said coldly.

The Blue Duck quickly backed down.

"No, ma'am. I reckon I'll go join the game."

"You'd better."

The Blue Duck strolled through an open door into a lighted room away from the Kid's window. There seemed to be several fellows in there, playing cards.

Somebody came riding right up to the front door. Not liking the look of the place despite the woman's presence, Pryor hunkered down in the shadows. Belle dropped her homely pursuits and reached a slim hand under her apron.

"Come in," Pryor heard her call out softly.

"Guess I'll sashay," the Rio Kid mused. "It's a purty mysterious place they run here!"

But he took a last look inside. The newcomer was dragging a limp, blanket-swathed figure with him.

"Oh, so it's you, Vance," the woman exclaimed.

The lean hombre had a lobster-red face, fierce and sharp, carrot-colored hair, long and shaggy under his Stetson. At his bony shanks rode two Frontier Model Colts. He grinned, showing a gap where a tooth was missing. Letting his heavy freight fall to the floor with a thud, he stepped over toward the woman.

The sight of the blanket-covered man made the Rio Kid jump. It might well be his friend Celestino. He must save the lad if Mireles had fallen into the hands of the rustlers. The tall man might have been one of the thieves they had been trailing.

Vance pulled a chunk of cured cowhide from inside his shirt and carelessly dropped it on the table. The horse-blanket covering the doubled-up figure did not stir. Pryor could not even see the boots.

"Say, yuh're shore a pretty woman, Belle," the sorrel-topped man remarked with a grin, seizing her hand. "I ain't knowed yuh long, but I've decided yuh're the girl for me. Any woman who kin roll a gun and her eyes as expert as you, deserves the best. Yuh're a widder. My wives is all dead or gone down the pike. Let's git spliced and throw in together. We kin go to hell and back."

The young woman hit him in the face with the flat of her hand. He recoiled, scowling.

"Sorreltop Vance," Belle said icily, "if you ever lay a hand on me again I'll let daylight through you. Any dealin's with you are strictly business, savvy?"

"Aw right," growled Vance.

He shrugged, swung and picked up the cowhide, sat down on a log seat. Drawing his bowie knife, he began to fashion something from the piece of cowhide, while Belle watched curiously. The Rio Kid awaited his opportunity.

"If yuh're cuttin' out that heart for a valentine for me," the woman said after a minute, "you better split it in half, Vance."

"It ain't for you, Belle. A pal asked me to make it." He finished the shaping, held it

33

up. The Kid noted that it was in the rough shape of a heart.

Vance stuck the finished product inside his shirt and reached for the whiskey.

"Now," said Belle, "since you're right at home and cozy, Sorreltop, how about lettin' me in on your little secret under the table there? Is it dead, alive or something else?"

"He ain't dead yet," Vance replied. "But he will be soon as Gonzales gits here, and trimmed with that there hide heart! The one reason he ain't finished off is that Gonzales made me promise to let him do it in his own fanciful way."

"You and that Mex pard of yours are goin' to run into some tall trouble one of these days," warned Belle.

"We kin take care of anything. Yuh got that stock ready to drive?"

"The steers are mostly in but I expect the boys along with a bunch of horses and some more cows by dawn. You can run 'em with you. I don't fancy keepin' stolen stuff around here too long. Of course you got the money?"

"Shore, shore." Sorreltop Vance patted his bulky middle. "Yuh'll git it on delivery, Belle."

The clever young woman, known to fame as Belle Starr, was in her twenties. She had great beauty and a tremendous attraction for men, not only of the outlaw class, but for every type of male. She never hesitated to use her charm to cheat and rob luckless victims who saw only her outward soft beauty.

The Rio Kid had heard of some of her exploits. He realized suddenly just who she was. Stories about Belle Shirley — her maiden name — had spread through the Armies in the Civil War. As a sixteen-year-old Missouri belle, she had led many Yankee officers into death traps. She had been acquainted with William Quantrill and set this ferocious guerilla leader on detachments of Federal troops. Then she had married a horsethief, Jim Reed, and followed him, helping to steal and kill.

Expert rider and first-class shot with a six-gun, Belle was becoming a legendary figure in Texas, her adopted home state. After Reed died by the gun of an officer who had trailed him, Belle had set up for herself and was doing brilliantly. It was plain that she was a source of supply for Vance and Gonzales.

"Now look here, Vance," Belle said, "you're mighty confident, but let me tell you this. One of my men rode in from Brownsville this morning. He claims the

Rangers are sendin' Captain McNelly down to the Rio Grande again to capture you cattle thieves."

"McNelly!" Sorreltop jumped up. "Why, damn that Ranger's hide, I'll nail it to Las Cuevas fence."

"You talk mighty big for a common stock thief. I heard that when McNelly was around Brownsville last year you hit the chaparral so fast it started a fire."

"We did move up-river to Las Cuevas on McNelly's account. But this time we're organized and it'll be diff'rent. Gen'ral Juan Flores kin muster two thousan' fightin' men. Money's pourin' in and we got a clear lane open to the Rio. The Army can't cross the Border after us, and we ain't expectin' trouble."

"Then you better start," insisted Belle. "McNelly's a real fightin' man, whatever else he may be." She looked around for the gun-belt she had been sewing on before Vance had entered. It had fallen to the floor. "I've dropped my sewin', Vance," she said.

"Huh? Well, pick it up," the redhead replied.

The Kid could see the angry flush spread over the woman's cheek. She whipped out a six-shooter. Surprised, Vance quailed under her furious, flashing eyes.

"You step over here and pick it up for me," ordered Belle. "I'll learn you how to treat a lady."

Sheepishly Sorreltop obeyed.

Pryor would have gone on his way had it not been for that bundle of humanity on the floor. Suddenly the hard muzzle of a gun rammed into his back.

"Reach!" a thin voice ordered.

The Rio Kid reached. Only death would have repaid him had he fought now. He preferred to wait for a better chance rather than be blown inside out. His hands went up. "March to the front door," growled the hombre who had crept up on him.

Belle and Vance heard the voice outside and drew guns.

"What's wrong there?" demanded the woman loudly.

"It's me, Belle," called the Kid's captor. "Jest caught a feller spyin' outside yore winder and I'm fetchin' him in."

Gun in his vitals, Bob Pryor walked around the house corner and entered the open door. Belle stared curiously at the handsome Rio Kid. Smooth-shaven, non-chalant, youthful, showing no alarm though death was upon him, Pryor drew the eyes of women.

"Yuh know him?" asked the thin-voice fellow still behind the Kid. "I'd've shot him, Belle, but I figgered he might be one of yore crowd."

"No, I don't know him," replied the woman.

Sorreltop Vance saw only an enemy and spy in the Kid. He ripped off Pryor's gun-belt and slung it back on the bunk. Viciously he lashed out at the Kid's mouth, driving him back against the wall. Red rage seized Pryor. He regained his footing, sprang at the redhead. But the limp bundle in the horse-blanket on the floor stirred and groaned.

The woman saved the good-looking, soldierly young man from instant death.

"Hold your guns, boys," she snapped. She had a pistol in her hand and her eyes shone with determination. Sorreltop knew she would shoot a man for failing to heed her. He swore, falling back from Pryor. The gunny who had taken the Kid grabbed Pryor's vest and yanked him back.

"Sit down, you," Belle told him.

Anger abating, the Kid shrugged, lowered himself to a soap-box. The men in the other room had left their game to gather in the doorway and watch. There were several of them, hard-faced fellows wearing guns strapped low on their hips.

The man who had captured him shut the wooden slab-door and stepped into the Kid's range of vision.

"How'd yuh come to nab him, Hardin?" asked Vance.

"I jest rode up the east trail," replied Hardin. "Happened to see him bob up against the winder. Left my bronc and crept up on him. Wasn't shore but what he might be one of yore men, Belle."

"No, I never saw him before," she replied.

"Me either," Vance agreed. "He's a spy, aw right."

The Rio Kid looked over the slight young man who had brought him in. Acquainted with the notorious as well as the famous of the West, Pryor had heard tell of John Wesley Hardin, said to be the worst killer of them all. The son of a Methodist preacher, Hardin had gone bad at an early age. He was shorter than the Kid, his clothes dirty and shabby. But his guns were in perfect order. If any man ever shot another just to see him kick, that was John Wesley Hardin.

"I've shore walked into a fine den of citizens," thought the Kid, though outwardly he showed nothing. He seemed as at ease as though there for a cup of tea.

"S'pose I take him outside, Belle," suggested John Wesley, "and rid yuh of his presence?"

"Wait," Belle said.

The bundle under the table straightened out some. From the corner of his eye, Pryor noted the great boots.

It was not Celestino. It was some unfortunate whom Sorreltop Vance had taken.

"Who are you, anyway?" the woman asked the Kid.

"Yuh wouldn't b'lieve me if I told yuh," Pryor replied. "But I ain't the sort who walks into a house jest any old way, Ma'am. Nor was my friend, Jim Reed. He often spoke of yore beauty, and I come to see yuh for myself. Reed didn't do yuh justice."

CHAPTER IV
THE KID ACTS

Pryor had never known Reed, Belle's first husband, and father of her two children. But he was playing for his life and knew he had made a beginning when he saw her eyes change. Belle had loved Reed and followed him through thick and thin. The Kid's compliment was spoken with real sincerity. He wasn't lying when he said Belle was attractive.

"So you know who I am," she said quickly. Her glance hardened. She was not sure just what this man before her was. He might be a spy after her. He might be, as he hinted, on the dodge, hunting sanctuary. "I knew most of Jim's pals, Mister, and you don't look like any of 'em."

The Rio Kid shrugged. "I was told that if I come here, I'd be safe for awhile. But then, I s'pose I shouldn't've b'lieved it. I on'y wished to be shore I was at the right place, Ma'am."

The men watched. The Kid's eyes had already taken in the single light on the table, a glass-chimneyed lamp with a round reservoir.

"We'll go through him," Belle started to say, and the Rio Kid made ready for a last play. Hidden cunningly under his arms were his spare guns and he did not mean to give them up without a fight.

John Wesley Hardin took a step toward him, paused, and swung toward the door.

"Someone comin', Belle."

The diversion gave the Kid another breathing spell. A voice sang out.

"It's Gonzales," Vance cried.

Xavier Gonzales, the thin vaquero chief, swaggered into the house. Out in the shadows a dozen or more of his Mexicans sat their hairy mustangs. Gonzales, clad in high-peaked, rimmed sombrero and velvet suit with bell-shaped trouser legs, swept the sombrero from his sleek black head and bowed.

"Senora, Senores! I salute you."

"Got a s'prise for yuh, Xavier," Vance said. "Look." He spurred the blanket-covered man by the table.

Gonzales bent down, loosed the rounds of rawhide lariat which had held the prisoner's legs and arms. He jerked the blanket away and gave a sibilant hiss as he recognized his enemy.

"Dan Worrell!" he cried. "Where you get heem, Vance?"

"The boss handed him over to me on my way up here," replied Sorreltop. "Yuh said yuh wanted him alive, and here he is."

The Rio Kid was glad enough that for the moment they forgot him. He took in the features of the big young fellow who pushed himself to a sitting position, feeling dazedly the blood that had congealed in his tow hair and run down onto his bronzed cheek. Worrell was a typical Texan, square and rugged of face. Pryor had no idea what the grudge was about but he could say for sure that Worrell was an honest man, if only because Xavier Gonzales and Vance were against him.

With a characteristic hissing breath Xavier Gonzales leaped forward and drove his knife into Worrell's cheek.

"Stop that, Gonzales," Worrell growled, pulling back.

"I teach you," screamed the vindictive bravo. "I teach you to keel my *amigos*. You woun' me, too!"

He jabbed with lightning-like rapidity at Worrell's eyes and cheeks. The Texan put up his hands to shield himself but Gonzales sought vengeance for the fight Worrell had dared to put up against the marauders of the Rio Grande.

Worrell tried to get to his feet. He nearly succeeded but the knife drove him back. The men in the doorway of the other room were laughing at the fun, although Belle did not seem much amused.

"You're making an awful mess, Gonzales," she said coldly. "S'pose you take him outside —"

"Watch it!" A sharp cry of warning came from the men in the doorway.

The Rio Kid had seized his moment. His hand flashed inside his shirt as he came up on his feet. John Wesley Hardin made his famous draw — fast as light, hand a blur. His speed was phenomenal, yet the Kid's gun roared right on top of his.

Bob Pryor felt the bite Hardin's slug took out of his boot. Feet spread wide, he had shot just in time to shatter the ace gunman's aim. His slug hit the cylinder of the big Frontier Model in Hardin's hand. The pistol left the man's fingers paralyzed. Like an echo to the connected shots, the Kid's second one blazed. The heavy bullet drilled the glass lamp, extinguishing the flame as though a black hat had been thrown over it.

Heavy boots immediately shook the flimsy building. Yells rang out, and the shrill scream of the woman. Something heavy hit the front door.

"There he goes, out the front," bellowed Sorreltop Vance.

John Wesley Hardin recovered instantly. He drew his spare pistol and fired at the door. Vance, too, was shooting that way. The Mexican bravo began screaming shrilly for help.

The Rio Kid had ducked as he made his shot at the lamp. He had thrown the heavy soap-box at the front door, dived under the table, scrambling past the young prisoner and Gonzales.

"Git out, pronto," he whispered.

Down low he made the open window and sprang clear through it. He landed on his shoulder, rolled, and came up running.

Pandemonium reigned inside, yells of warning and advice.

"He went out the window. I saw him!" screamed Belle.

A moment too late the window streamed lead. But the Rio Kid had ducked up the canyon and was streaking for the slide. Somewhere out in the darkness was Saber. Gonzales' bravos were riding in, though, blocking the entrance.

Pryor leaped over the little brook in one long jump. The bawling of imprisoned steers deafened him, yet did not prevent him from hearing the sounds of pursuit.

He looked back over his hunched shoulders. Wild bullets were coming his way. Someone had glimpsed him jump the brook.

"There he goes!"

"Like to pull Worrell outa that," Pryor grunted.

He had liked the looks of the young Texan. Unhorsed as he was, he figured on climbing the rock slide and making the chaparral above. He had a few bullets in his spare guns, but had lost his belt and expensive Army Colts.

He reached the slide. Close to the big corrals, he looked across the massed, long-horned steers. Then he glanced back again at the pursuit. They were organizing to come after him with rifles and torches.

"Damn their hides," he muttered. "Mebbe it'll bother 'em. Anyways, I want my guns, and they'll kill Worrell!"

Instead of continuing to escape, Bob Pryor quickly began pulling down the thick pole-bars that held in the cattle. Then he hustled to the side of the ravine, over their heads, and began screeching, throwing rocks.

He even wasted two of his precious bullets.

It took the leaders no time at all to start rolling. They were only looking for an excuse to stampede and the Rio Kid, knowing cattle, gave them more than enough reason. Whooping like a mad Indian, throwing sharp rocks that cut and startled the big animals, he saw his ruse succeed as the steers lumbered beneath him down the narrow *barranca.*

He egged them on until they were galloping at full-tilt out the mouth of the ravine. The gunnies in pursuit of the Kid had to jump for the safety of the house or take to the trees up the sides. Dust rolled up and the ground shook under the beating hoofs.

"Stop 'em!"

Above the din rose the frantic cry. A small fortune in beef was leaving Belle's premises, and every available hand rushed outside to attempt to break the stampede.

The Rio Kid paused, spitting dirt from his mouth. The corral, which had been formed by blocking off the upper ravine, rapidly emptied.

In the drag dust, the Kid jumped down and started along the trail of the excited beeves who had driven everything on before them. He crossed the brook, gun in hand, watching for trouble. Ducking up under the window, he looked into the front room. It was again lighted by a candle brought from the other side.

Xavier Gonzales had his knife to Dan Worrell's throat. Belle stood at the front door, watching the men as they sought to break the stampede.

"Drop the knife, Gonzales," the Rio Kid yelled above the uproar.

The Mexican jumped. He swung, eyes flashing hatred.

"Ees ze othair —" he began.

Worrell leaped to his feet, hope coming into his young face. He reached for Gonzales, ripped away the bowie knife. With one powerful hand, he lifted the Mexican bravo and flung him bodily against the wall. Belle screamed, alarm in her pretty face.

"Hustle, Worrell," shouted Pryor. "No time for that."

The catlike Mexican had rolled off the wall, then recovered and was reaching for his gun. He pulled one from a fancy trimmed holster and started it up. Pryor had to shoot, and he sent the bravo rolling again, screeching with anguish.

In the next moment, Dan Worrell was squeezing out the window, dropping at the Rio Kid's feet.

A bullet roared right over Pryor's head. It came from Belle's six-shooter. But he would not fight a woman, no matter what kind. Calling to Worrell to follow, he gave shrill whistles over his shoulder as he ran.

If the dun heard, they should bring Saber running. A couple of Belle's followers burst around the back of the house, saw the two streaking for the rock slide and began firing after them. Gun flashes slashed through the black dust and the night, screaming dangerously close to the swift-moving fugitives.

They reached the bottom of the rock slide, the only way up the cliff without ropes.

"Here, Worrell, take this, but don't use it 'less yuh hafta. We're mighty short on ammunition." He pressed his pistol into Dan's big hand, and drew his second spare.

"Thanks, Mister. I dunno who yuh are but yuh shore showed at a most convenient time," gasped Worrell. Only his youth and tremendous strength made it possible for him to overcome the torture in such short order.

Now there was no time to waste. Yells and the reports of shotguns and Colts probed for the pair as they started working up the rock slide. If Saber had heard the Kid's whistling call, he was unable to reach his master. Perhaps he had been swept up by the stampeding cattle and was miles away in the brush by this time. But the Kid knew he would return to the vicinity where he had last seen his master. Pryor could not stay close to the den of stock thieves. A number of Belle's men emerged from the south chaparral and started for them.

Dan Worrell followed the lithe Rio Kid who scaled the steep, sliding rocks like a mountain goat ahead of him. He stuck the pistol the Kid had passed him into his trousers belt, for he needed both hands to pull himself up the steps of eroded stone.

A fleet runner reached the bottom of the slide before Worrell could scramble up. The Kid had turned. On one knee, he was looking down into the *barranca*. A double-barreled shotgun was aimed at Dan's back, for he was climbing painfully up the final rise.

Chapter V
The Black Heart
Again

Right by Worrell's ear blasted the Rio Kid's gun. The flash blinded him and his eardrums banged with the echoes. He heard a shriek of pain. The shotgun roared. But the pellets came nowhere near him, and then he was up beside the man who had snatched him from death.

Others were coming up, shooting and ordering them to stop. But they dived into the woods and ran from the deep ravine. For awhile they could see over their shoulders the light in Belle's house. By that and the stars they zigzagged to elude their furious enemies in the darkness.

For over an hour the two young men kept going, despite the burning of their throats, the gasping of their tortured lungs. Impeded by the heavy clothing they wore in riding the thorned chaparral, they swung in and out through the narrow lanes of the wilderness.

At last Dan Worrell stopped.

"Can't — go — another — step —" he gasped, and sank face down on the warm earth.

The Rio Kid was too out of breath to reply. He threw himself down and for a few minutes they simply fought to recover their spent wind.

Worrell finally sat up. He could see, by the silver moonlight streaking through gaps in the foliage, the oval of the Rio Kid's face.

"Mister," he observed, "I still can't see how yuh got outa there yoreself, let alone drag me with yuh!"

"I couldn't've done it," the Kid replied, "but that yuh were there and made a sort of a diversion, Worrell. What's Sorreltop Vance got against yuh?"

The quiet voice of his savior, the way the lithe young fellow conducted himself in action, had deeply impressed Dan Worrell. He felt the power of the commander and the affection of a comrade who would go to the death for a friend.

"Yuh know my name," Dan remarked, "but though I'm feelin' mighty grateful, I don't savvy yores."

"Name is Bob Pryor. Sometimes they call me the Rio Kid."

"The Rio Kid! Say, yuh're the feller

52

busted up that gang across the Pecos. And I heard tell yuh'd been up in Kansas, workin' as a marshal in Ellsworth!"

The Kid nodded. He squatted on his haunches, fishing around for a cigarette paper to roll himself a smoke.

Worrell remembered when he was recovering from the blow he had received from behind. He had heard vaguely some of Pryor's attempt to pass himself off as a fugitive so as to turn the wrath of John Wesley Hardin and Belle Starr. But now he fully believed what his new friend told him. He could not think anything else after what Pryor had done for him.

"That dirty Gonzales would've tortured me to death, if yuh hadn't got me outa there, Kid."

"What did they have it in for yuh about?" repeated Pryor.

"It's a long story," Worrell replied, "but I'll try to tell it fast, Pryor. I owned a little spread near the Rio, and was jest gittin' her well started. Well, I got a girl who promised to marry me when I have a home for her. I had it 'bout done when them cattle thieves from Las Cuevas started raidin' the whole country. I managed to fight 'em off for awhile. Shot up some of Gonzales' bravos. I even nicked Gonzales hisself but they drove me out, burnt my place and run off my stock."

He clenched his teeth, eyes burning with the hideous memory.

"They're shore hawgs for cattle and horses, ain't they?" Pryor grunted. "We run into a pack of 'em headin' for Belle's, on the trail from Kansas. That's how I happened to strike that hideout."

"Yeah, yuh see it's this here Cuban war for independence. There's a bottomless market for beef and cavalry mounts. Why, steers're eighteen dollars a head right now, any kind at all! Thousands of Mexes were makin' money, only they've run short of stock across the Rio and thieves're hittin' way up into Texas. The Rangers chased 'em off down Brownsville way. Yuh know they was hittin' the King Ranch there awful hard, and Cap'n Richard King was on their trails, too.

"Then they moved further upriver, where there's General Juan Flores Salinas. He owns Las Cuevas, a Mex village with a couple thousand people in it, set some three miles back from the Rio. Gonzales and Vance work from there, I'm shore of that. They kin muster any number of vaqueros, Mexes and renegades. It's a one-way trail for plenty of Texas cattle, Kid. I dunno what's goin' to happen if somethin' ain't done to stop it. They've been killin' and burnin' where anybody dares scrap back."

"I hear Cap'n McNelly's on his way to these parts."

Worrell slapped his big thigh. "I hope so! It's time. If he does come, I'm goin' to try to join up with him. No use to set up a ranch in these parts now."

All Worrell's small savings had gone into his ranch. He would not ask Conchita to marry him until he could support her properly. But he wanted to clean the country of all rustlers.

"And how'd Sorreltop Vance happen to catch yuh?" his companion inquired, the red glow of his cigarette lighting the keen, handsome face, bronzed with strength and health.

"Huh! I'd like to know myself, Kid. I rode to Smithville — that's where this here young lady lives — the night they burnt me out. There was some trouble there, and I hung around the Purcells' store. George Purcell is Conchita's dad. I reported to the law, and we figgered on gittin' up a company of volunteers to fight the thieves. I was goin' from house to house yestiddy, tryin' to stir folks up. But there's been sev'ral mysterious killin's there. Funny, the murderer leaves a chunk of cowhide cut in the shape of a black heart near his victim!"

Worrell missed the widening of the Rio Kid's eyes. Dan had been unconscious, wrapped in the horse blanket, when Vance had made that heart at Belle's.

"Go on," growled Pryor.

"Well, folks're afraid to leave home long, for fear somebody'll be killed by this Black Heart hombre. Jest after dark last night I was walkin' back to the Purcells'. Some sidewinder slipped out of an alley and hit me such a clip over the head I never knowed what happened till I woke up in that thieves' den. Mebbe it was Vance who came to town secret-like to take me. Xavier Gonzales was honin' for revenge on me, not on'y for his own sport but to show other Texans not to dare shoot his bravos."

Dan Worrell's companion seemed to be turning all this over in his mind. At last the Rio Kid spoke. "I was on my way to Smithville, Worrell. I got separated from a friend of mine on the way here, and I reckon he'll head there."

"Good. We kin head for there together." Worrell couldn't think of another hombre he would prefer to ride the river with.

"I ain't eager to give up my guns. They're pets of mine," Pryor remarked. "However, first we need to git horses."

"Any idee where we are?" asked Dan.

"We're mebbe twenty-five miles northwest of Smithville," Pryor answered laconically.

"Say, I'll bet that *barranca's* one they call Hell's Gate. I been to it once, huntin' wild cattle, but there wasn't a shack there then."

"Reckon that hideout was tossed up to make money on the Cuban beef market. But c'mon, we want to git away from here. In the daylight they kin hunt us out. They'll savvy we'll tell the law on 'em if we git clear."

"Walkin's awful slow. Yuh reckon we could go back and steal a couple horses from them outlaws?"

The Kid shook his head. "Not tonight. They're on the lookout and primed. But I got an idee, if we kin make the cross trail in time. Let's go."

Dan heaved up his big body, shook himself, wiped dirt and sweat from his face. He would follow the Kid anywhere.

Pryor took the lead, heading south. From the east they heard a pistol shot, but the sound was faint. They shoved on, and two hours later broke onto a beaten trail running east to west. Dan Worrell thought that if they followed this to the left it would bring them to the thieves' hideout.

The Rio Kid was down on hands and knees, feeling the sod of the track through the wilderness.

"Okay," he announced. "They ain't been by yet. Now listen. I told yuh my friend and me run into the tail end of some stock thieves, on our way from Kansas. They was some distance off, comin' due south. I know now they couldn't work their cows and horses down the *barranca,* so they was makin' for this trail. I heard Belle say they was due round dawn. They ought to be along here any time. I figger on gettin' us a couple horses, Worrell."

"I'm with yuh."

"Then take the south side and I'll take the other. We'll let them git by, then hit the rear guard, savvy?"

An hour later, Dan Worrell caught the faint sound of approaching hoofs. The noise grew in volume. He knew that there were many horses and beeves, taken in raids to the north. Driving such herds was slower than straight riding. The animals would break off to the flanks, forcing a stop, and they insisted on halting to rest and drink.

The van riders appeared around the bend in the trail. Worrell, down low behind the inky shadows of mesquite bushes, glimpsed the hard faces of the leaders. Behind them, at a slow trot, came the steers, crushing along, bumping against each other in the constricted way. Most of them were three-year olds, with some bulls and tough cows, long of horn and leg and able to outrace a horse. The other side of the trail, where the Kid was hiding, was obscured by the dust they raised.

Muscles tensed, Dan Worrell waited for the Rio Kid's signal. It seemed a long time before the crushing cattle, bawling and horning each other, finally passed. Then came the horses, hairy mustangs some of them, but others clearly branded with foot-high sears showing they were ranch stock from some northern outfit. Held back by the crush of steers ahead, the mustangs walked and trotted, skilfully herded by the expert riders. Well-mounted on trained horses, they were alert for any sudden turn-off or stampede.

The mustangs finally got past the spot where Dan Worrell was hidden. The dust was thick as a curtain. In the drag, bandannas raised against the choking alkali, came four heavily armed hombres. They were about fifty yards behind the stock. Still the Rio Kid stayed where he was and the four swung the turn.

"Wonder what he's thinkin' of," muttered

Worrell.

He figured the quartet was the last of them. But then his keen ears caught the clop-clop of more shod hoofs in the trail.

Here came the rear guard, watching for trailing ranchers or law officers who had been able to follow the sign this far. No doubt they had a secret turn-off from the main road. They must have hidden their tracks with blankets weighted with stones, and setting up walls of thornbrush as a screen.

There were three in the extreme rear. The young rancher could see the black holstered pistols and the moonlight glittering on their carbines.

The first went by. Then Worrell saw the Rio Kid spring out of the bush and unerringly seize the reins of the startled mustang.

Worrell plunged after the Kid. With one hand he got the bridle reins. With the other he tore at the astounded rider. Almost home, they had all begun to relax, expecting trouble only from the rear.

Curses sputtered from both riders. The free one whirled his horse, whipped out his Colt. With a shout, he spurred back to assist his pals.

The Kid had his hands full with the burly hombre he had jumped. Dan Worrell knew that to succeed they must make it fast. He had the strength of a grizzly in his great arms. He ripped his man out of his leather and threw him bodily into the mesquite. The horse danced in a circle from him but he kept an iron hold on the reins. An instant later he vaulted into the saddle.

The Kid's gun snapped. The man he had attacked was yanking a Colt on him. Worrell saw the flash of the moonlight on its barrel. Pryor yanked then. The hombre collapsed, slid out of his leather, and the Rio Kid hastily sought to mount.

In the darkness the third outlaw was almost upon Pryor. Worrell, jerking on his right rein, whirled his mustang around to stop the sudden charge. A six-shooter stabbed through the night. Horrified, Worrell saw the Kid go down, horse and all, as the gunman shot a second time.

"Damn yuh," snarled Worrell, fighting blood up.

He thought the Kid dead. The path was cleared between the gunny and himself. He whipped out the gun Pryor had given him. The rider had a Colt turned on him.

Worrell aimed and fired, all in one smooth motion. But the hammer of the six-gun clicked metallically on a spent shell.

CHAPTER VI
THE KID RETURNS

With a curse, Worrell hurled the gun at the approaching enemy. It caught him in the face. His Colt barked but his aim had been spoiled by Worrell's ruse.

Heels drumming the excited mustang's ribs, Worrell rode down on him. The mustangs collided. Worrell snatched the gunny off his leather, but his giant grip still held the outlaw's arm. He felt a bone snap, heard his helpless captive squeal like an injured pig. And then the revolver fell useless from the limp hand.

"Yuh skunk!" growled Worrell. "Shoot my pard, will yuh?"

He raised the man, who was not a small customer and smashed him with all his might to the ground. The gunny lay still, head doubled under him. Dan Worrell pulled the rein, eyes glowing fire.

With an oath of joy he saw that the Rio Kid was up. Pryor had seized the reins of the third horse. The animal he had been on lay dead in the trail.

"Let's ride," gasped the Rio Kid. "Here come the rest!"

Yells and gunshots told them that the quartet in the drag were hustling back to assist their friends. Pivoting, the two comrades rode away hell-for-leather.

"You're hurt, Rio Kid?" Worrell called, when they had made a quarter mile. "Yuh don't ride like it."

"Got a singe along my leg," the Kid replied. "The bullet drove past my thigh and hit that mustang in the heart."

Taking to the brush, the Kid turned around entirely. They headed parallel with the narrow trail that led to Belle Starr's place.

In the gray dawn they thought they were nearing the hideout. But from this direction and every way except when close upon the *barranca* in the wild chaparral, the shack was screened from spying eyes.

They cut several cattle trails. On these Gonzales and Vance probably drove their stolen cattle south for the Rio Grande and Las Cuevas.

Suddenly the quick beat of a mustang's hoofs caused them to swing in their leather, ready for battle. The Kid's hand flew to the

Colt he had stuck in his belt.

A grayish shape galloped, snorting with rage, from the north chaparral. The wind had carried the Rio Kid's scent to the dun. Saber charged furiously at the reddish mustang the Kid was on, biting a chunk of hairy hide out of the animal's flank and rearing up to strike out viciously with his forehoofs.

"Why, that horse is loco!" cried Worrell, not knowing the Kid's pet.

"Stop, cut it out, Saber," roared the Rio Kid.

But he found the dun's jealousy something to grin at. Dan Worrell shoved in and began beating the dun off with the quirt which had been hanging from the saddle-horn.

The brick-colored horse reared high on his hind legs, ears laid back and big yellow teeth bared in a snarl. Pryor let go and slid off, jumping out of range of the lashing hoofs. The red horse immediately dashed away into the mesquite with the black-striped dun following with vicious nips. The Kid quickly whistled, "Said the Big Black Charger." Saber reluctantly gave up the chase and came trotting back, lifting his forelegs high in triumph.

Bob Pryor swung into his familiar saddle, smiled at the astounded Worrell.

"He's my horse," he explained, as the young rancher stared open-mouthed at the dun's sudden gentling under his master's hand. "He don't fancy I ride any other mustang and figgers on makin' it plain."

"Well, dang my hide. It beats all," exclaimed Dan.

He found he must keep his black at a respectful distance, for Saber was an equine bully when it came to other mustangs. Trained to forage and take care of himself throughout the Civil War, and as a cavalryman's fighting comrade, the dun would allow no one but Pryor to touch him unless the Rio Kid ordered him to behave.

They rode on but the Kid kept looking north toward the shack. He wanted his guns and he hated to run from trouble. Worrell began telling him about Conchita and her father.

"They're fine folks, salt of the earth."

The dun rippled his hide, softly snorted. The Kid pulled up, Worrell following suit.

"Somethin' comin'," warned Pryor. "Git back — quick!"

In the nick of time the two rode behind dense mesquite brush. Dismounting, Worrell kept his big hand on his mustang's muzzle to prevent the beast from neighing.

The Kid silently signaled his friend,

dropped Saber's rein and began worming closer to the trail. The slightest warning would turn enemy guns against them in the bright light of the new day.

Bob Pryor had heard Worrell's talk of his sweetheart, of his ambition to provide a good home for her. At the same time he felt admiration for the honest young rancher, he also experienced a tinge of envy. Such a goal would never satisfy him and he often wished it would. The exciting years of the Civil War had dislocated the lives of millions of young men. Some managed to work back into the general run of life. Others, like the Rio Kid, sought excitement on the Frontier.

The war had completely changed Pryor. His parents had died during it, and many of his friends in Texas were now gone. He had found it impossible to settle down to the tameness of civilization. The restless urging of his nature forced him to reckless pursuits. Never staying long in one spot, the Kid rode the vast West, and was known from Kansas to the Border as a first-class fighting man, always ready to give a hand to the helpless and needy.

Men lived on the Frontier for several reasons. Land hunger was the chief one. A desire for quick riches was another, and usually a vain one. On their heels came the predatory, some to escape the law in the States, some to rob and kill where the law could not reach.

The Kid enjoyed this roaming existence. When bored, he could always find trouble. Gunmen in the West gloried in shooting aces like the Kid so they could boast of it. And yet at times he did envy a simple fellow like Worrell. Plenty of women, good and bad, had smiled on the Kid, but he hadn't yet found one who could hold him from the life he led.

Now, flat in the bushes along the trail, the Rio Kid saw the steers and horses being driven for the Rio Grande. He glimpsed Sorreltop Vance, Xavier Gonzales, looking sour and with wounds bandaged, injuries dealt him by the Kid. Also, he observed some of the hombres who had been at Belle's, evidently helping the drive.

"Reckon they rounded up as many as they could and wanta git 'em outa there, quick. Figger we'll call in the law."

There wouldn't be many left at Belle's. Probably others of her followers were still out hunting the rest of the stampeded stock.

He waited till the cavalcade hustled by. Then he returned to Worrell.

"Look, Dan," the Kid said quickly. "You ride to Smithville and tell the sheriff 'bout this. I'll tell yuh somethin'. While I was peekin' in at Belle's, I seen Sorreltop Vance carve a heart out of cowhide. He meant to leave it on yore corpse."

Dan Worrell jumped. "Huh? Why, them Black Heart murders have got us so upset we're jest about crazy — So it's Vance!"

"Mebbe. Though he said a pard had asked him to do it. I figger on gittin' Vance some time soon. He's gone south but he'll be back. I reckon he could be made to talk if he's captured."

"Wait'll Sheriff Carr hears of this. It may clean up the whole business."

"Mebbe. I'd like to help yuh and the folks in these parts, Worrell."

"Thanks, Kid. S'pose we hustle and call in Sheriff Carr?"

Pryor shook his head. "I'm goin' back to Belle's and try to git my guns. Besides, I wanta see what this gang of robbers does between now and when the sheriff comes."

He convinced Worrell that it was best for Dan to leave him and head for Smithville.

Alone, the Rio Kid swung back for the shack. Dismounting close to the building, he crept forward and reconnoitered from the bush. There was a faint smoke spiral coming from the stone chimney. He smelled coffee and frying beef in the air and he was hungry. He saw nothing but a couple of horses in sight.

Belle came out the front door, a bucket in her hand. She went to the stream and washed herself, then scooped up a bucket of water and started back to the hut.

"She wouldn't tote that if there was any man round to do it for her," decided the Kid.

At the proper moment he rose up and hurried toward her. She caught the sound of his light steps, looked toward him, startled as a deer. But she held the pail in her right hand and had to drop it, to reach the gun strapped under her apron.

The Kid was up to her by that time. In a swift tussle he took away her pistol and stuck it in his belt. She fought him like a tigress, struggling in his steel grip, and he was scratched and kicked. But he wouldn't hurt a woman, and once he had taken her gun out of harm's way, he stepped away from her.

"Take it easy, Belle," he drawled. "I don't aim to do yuh any harm. Jest wanted to tote the bucket for yuh."

"Yuh — you —" She was furious. But, disarmed, the feminine cunning with which she was so richly endowed came to the fore.

The Kid picked up the spilled pail, went

and filled it again, and she watched his lithe, handsome figure. Presently her eyes softened as the young man grinned at her. She led the way inside the shack. The Kid put down the bucket.

On the rough table stood breakfast, coffee in a pot, strips of beef, baked biscuits, and it looked mighty appetizing to the Rio Kid. His guns hung from a peg and he went and strapped them on.

Pryor pulled out a chair, and gallantly offered it to Belle. She looked at him, her eyes troubled, but then sat down. The Rio Kid took a seat opposite her.

"I could use a cuppa coffee, Miss Belle," he said softly.

She poured him a tin mugful, and cool as a cucumber, the Kid began to eat and drink.

Belle was silent, stunned by the way the Kid acted, yet impressed by his chivalry.

"You've got your nerve with you," she remarked at last. "You never really knew Jim, did you?"

"No, Ma'am, but I heard tell of him and you. That's one reason I come back. I lied 'bout knowin' yore husband but — Well, I wasn't lyin' when I said yuh was mighty purty. My name's Bob Pryor. They call me the Rio Kid."

Belle kept looking at him. "I've heard of

you. And what do you expect to gain by comin' here, Rio Kid?" she demanded.

"Main reason is I intend gittin' yuh outa this, Belle. It's no place for a woman. I'm goin' to start yuh on yore way. Yuh know the Rangers're headin' here, and I mean to stay around myself. There's big trouble brewin'. Yuh know anything of this Black Heart murder business?"

She shrugged. She would never betray a fellow criminal.

"So you think you can scare me out?" she asked.

"Nope, but yuh're smart as well as good lookin'. Soon as breakfast's done I'll saddle yuh a horse and see yuh git goin'. I don't fancy slingin' guns where a woman's concerned — any kind of a woman." The Kid looked straight into her eyes and she dropped her gaze.

"Then you don't aim to turn me over to the law?"

"No, Ma'am. All I want is for you to git outa this mess. Yuh kept yore bunch from killin' me before. I'm grateful for that." The Rio Kid had consumed a hearty meal, washing it down with tin mugs of coffee, and as he stood up he felt a lot better. "S'pose we leave the dishes to the Blue Duck and Hardin?" he drawled. "Pack yore duds and we'll start. I'll ride a way with yuh."

"It's might good of you, Rio Kid," she said, voice loud.

She sprang up, put her arms round his neck — and kissed him!

Chapter VII
Night Attack

Instantly Pryor was suspicious. He knew her ways. But before he could push her from him, John Wesley Hardin jumped through the door. Sitting close to the open window, Belle had evidently caught some slight sound of his approach, had made a diversion to fool the Kid.

"Stand away from him, Belle," snarled Hardin, gun leveled. "I'll let the daylight through his hide!"

The Kid was ready to fight. Hardin couldn't fire without taking a chance on hitting Belle, though he had the advantage of the draw. On the other hand, Pryor wasn't the sort to shield himself at a woman's peril. He was about to leap aside and shoot it out when she cried:

"Keep where you are, Rio Kid! The Blue Duck's at the back —"

He glanced around, saw that more of Belle's gunnies were coming through. Death was upon him. But a smile turned up the reckless Kid's lips as he faced it.

Belle took command of the situation.

"You boys put up your guns, pronto," she ordered. "The Rio Kid's a friend of mine."

"The Rio Kid!" exclaimed Hardin, scowling. "Say, I've heard tell of you. I'll duel yuh, Kid, draw for draw."

"That suits me," Pryor replied coldly.

"Shut up, both of you fools," ordered Belle. "Put up those guns, I say."

When her own men obeyed, she spoke to Pryor.

"Let me tell you this. I'm not afraid of you or the Rangers. But I reckon your advice is good. There's goin' to be hell to pay on the Border and so I'm on my way. Get out of here, Rio Kid, and stay away from us, savvy? I'll head for the Territory as soon as I'm packed."

"Are yuh gone loco, Belle?" shouted Hardin furiously. "Yuh fool, he'll fetch the law up here and spoil this hideout."

"Mind your language in front of a lady," Belle replied icily. "The big fellow Vance brought here must be well on his way to Smithville by now. He'll give the alarm. We just got paid for a big bunch and we're clear. I'm leaving. I don't like to buck the

Texas Rangers and — Well, the Rio Kid means to go after the rustlers, too."

"Gimme a shot at him," growled Hardin, "and he won't go anywhere but to hell. He can't scare me out and neither kin Mc-Nelly!"

Belle frowned angrily at the killer.

"Come on, Rio Kid. You're the best man in the place! Go for your horse."

Bob Pryor shrugged. He strolled for the front door, and Belle went with him. Her own men knew better than to cross her. John Hardin, evidently newly joined, would shoot if he had the chance, but she gave him none.

Guns strapped on, the Kid walked out of the shack, and Belle accompanied him across the clearing to the brush, where Saber stood hidden.

"Adios, Rio Kid," said Belle softly.

Pryor looked down at her. He knew her for the violent Frontier Amazon that she was, alluring to men, but a devil with a gun and no scruples, a thief and consort of thieves. Had it not been that the handsome young Kid had touched a chord in her feminine heart, he would be dead, as were so many others who had come under her spell. Just the same, Pryor bent and kissed her, then turned to hurry to the dun.

The men watched surlily from the shack. Belle stood where she was, looking after him.

The Kid mounted, disappeared east at a rapid clip. But he didn't ride far. After awhile he stopped, swung his horse, and started back. He crept in to see what the gang would do.

Men were straggling in with small bunches of the stampeded stock they had rounded up. Pryor took it easy in the shade for a couple of hours. Then he saw Belle come out, wearing a riding skirt and hat, boots on, quirt swinging jauntily from her wrist. The Blue Duck, one of her outlaw sycophants and admirers, followed her, toting a couple of heavy bags which he roped across the pack-horse's back. Then the Blue Duck and Belle mounted and rode west. The rest of the men stayed at the shack, though their horses were saddled.

The beat of hoofs caused the Kid to look east. A rider on a lathered mustang flashed past and pulled up at the shack. The Kid heard him call to Hardin and the men who came out.

"Git goin', boys! The chief says to move fast. Dan Worrell's got back to town and the sheriff's posse's on its way here!"

Quickly the gang took what they wanted

76

and hustled southwest into the chaparral.

There were too many of the desperadoes for the Kid to capture alone. He got Saber and rode east. Worrell should have reached Smithville before noon. If the posse had started within a half hour, they should be up before long.

But he had ridden some distance before he sighted them coming along the trail. The leader suddenly saw the Kid coming. He threw up a rifle and fired at Pryor. The bullet cut a chunk of felt out of the Kid's Stetson.

Pryor spurred sideward against the brush wall. Saber crashed through and the fusillade roared within a yard of them.

Dan Worrell, madly spurring up, was bellowing.

"That's not one of 'em, Sheriff. That's my friend, the Rio Kid, I told yuh 'bout."

The sheriff sang out, rode forward.

"Sorry, Mister Rio Kid! Thought yuh was one of them rustlers."

Pryor pushed back to the road. He took in the loose-jointed, powerful sheriff. Carr had the appearance of a good fighting man. His blue shirt was stained with sweat, under the flapping vest on which his star was pinned. Browned-steel guns rode high on his hips.

The officer looked over the lithe Kid. What Pryor had gone through had destroyed some of his bandbox appearance. Strangers were objects of suspicion on the frontier.

"Meet Bob Pryor, Sheriff Carr. This man saved me at Belle's. He seen Sorreltop Vance carve a heart outa cured hide."

"Vance and Gonzales were buyin' stolen stock from that gang," drawled the Kid. "They've pulled out now, Sheriff. Belle's gone back to Indian Territory, and Hardin and the rest hit into the southwest brush. They got a mighty long start. Somebody come and warned 'em yuh was on yore way."

Carr swore, rapped out orders. His posse, a couple of dozen men from Smithville, followed him forward. Pryor didn't fancy such a wild-goose chase. The chaparral was crossed and crisscrossed by thousands of hoofs that would hide rustlers' tracks from view.

"I'm headin' on to Smithville, Dan," he told his big friend. "I'm plumb wore out."

"I'll ride with yuh," Worrell replied.

He spoke to one of the possemen who was passing, and the Kid and Dan took the trail east. Both were exhausted, they had been in action for two days with no break.

They were not far from the town when

Saber quivered and gave a soft sniff of warning.

"Somebody comin'," Pryor said.

A disreputable Mexican pushed a hairy, run-down pinto from a patch of woods to the south and trotted toward them.

"Looks like one of Gonzales' men," Worrell grunted.

The Mex was bent over. He wore a dirty cape loose around his body. His face was smeared with dust and red clay, his battered sombrero pulled low over his eyes. He came right up to them and the Rio Kid watched him, a wrinkle in his forehead.

"Senores!" the vaquero said gruffly. "You see ze hombre zey call ze Rio Keed?"

Worrell started over as though to take part in any trouble. Pryor's face cleared and he grinned.

"Celestino! I'd never've known yuh in that rig. Yuh okay?"

"*Si*, my general. I come to hunt you. I was sure you rode ahead but no, you had not reach' Smeethville. My wound was nozzin', ees heal well. I talk weeth my frien's in town —" He broke off, looked at Worrell.

" 'Scuse me, Dan," said the Kid. "Wait for me."

He pushed Saber after the Mexican.

"I am happee you are okay, General. I was

worry' when you deedn't come."

"What yuh find out?"

"Zere ees beeg trouble here. Some killers zey call ze 'Black Heart.' Zey scare my people."

"I ran into that." Pryor quickly told Mireles what had occurred, of Vance and the cowhide heart at Belle's. "He runs with Gonzales, who's hooked up with Las Cuevas, across the Rio."

"I won't forget Senor Vance."

"Why the getup?" Pryor demanded.

"When I had foun' you, General, I meant to ride on to Las Cuevas, to learn more of ze Black Heart murders zere. Zey are connec' weeth ze cattle thievery, I am sure."

"Reckon yuh're right. These folks 'round here need help, Celestino, and I mean to give it to 'em. Wait and I'll ride with yuh."

"No, no," cried Mireles. "Please, General. Ees too dangerous for you to go to Las Cuevas."

That wasn't the way to stop the Kid and Celestino hurried on. "I mean, dangerous for me to hav' you weeth me. A *gringo* would be watch'."

Pryor knew what a genius Mireles was at working among his own people. As Celestino said, an American down there would stir them up like a giant beehive.

"Okay, then. Watch yore hide and I'll be waitin' to hear from yuh. If I come up with Vance or Gonzales I'll hold 'em, *Adios.*"

"*Hasta Luego,* General."

Mireles waved his slim brown hand, pivoted his hairy mount. He disappeared in the bush, aiming for Las Cuevas crossing on the Rio Grande.

Shortly after leaving Mireles, the Kid and Worrell went down a slope into the valley in which stood Smithville. Near the chaparral-fringed creek, they splashed across the stream, and cantered their tired horses into the Texas town.

Pryor took in the settlement. It was like so many other Southwest towns, surrounded by thorned bush, buildings of adobe and boards, built around a big, bare plaza. He noted the Mexican quarter, a jail with thick brick walls and barred window, sheriff's quarters at one end. There were three saloons. One of the general stores was George Purcell's big building. The other was a Mexican's, and outside it hung long red peppers and drying fruits.

"That's where Conchita lives," said Worrell, indicating the flat-roofed, roomy building.

The Kid trailed Worrell over to Purcell's large store. The thick-set Purcell, introduced to the Rio Kid, sang out. Conchita come from the living quarters in the rear.

"Oh, Dan, I'm glad you're back," she cried, kissing him. "I hated to see you ride off with the posse, after your narrow escape. I've been worried about you."

The Kid looked over the girl. She was very beautiful, lived up to Worrell's enthusiastic description. Arm around her, Dan beckoned to Pryor.

"This is the Rio Kid, who saved my life," Worrell told her.

Conchita seized Pryor's hand, and kissed it.

"I'll never forget that you snatched Dan from death!"

The Rio Kid smiled it off. George Purcell, white canvas apron over his clothes, wide smile on his broad face, told them to make themselves at home. They went back with Conchita.

The posse had not yet returned when darkness fell over the town. After supper, Worrell and the Kid decided to go to bed. There was a shack right behind the store with a couple of bunks. It didn't take them long to get to sleep. . . .

The Kid snapped awake with a start. The scream of a woman came from the big building. Shots began banging in the night, and the Kid leaped to his feet, grabbing his guns. Dan Worrell was right behind him. Together they ran out.

A number of dark figures raced around Purcell's. Blasting gunfire ripped from the loopholed windows.

Guns roaring, clearing a way to the half open door, the Kid and Worrell made it fast.

A Mexican in sombrero, face masked, was dragging Conchita toward the door!

CHAPTER VIII
BLACK HEART
MURDER

The Kid's gun blasted a slug through another masked hombre who swung around as they came in. Worrell sprang past him, got hold of the man who had dared touch Conchita. Strong as an ox, Worrell tore the Mex away and dashed him against the wall. The vaquero screamed, reaching for his knife. But Pryor shot him through the eye, killing him instantly.

Purcell was evidently busy on his own account up front. They heard the roaring guns, shouts of fighting men. A couple more Mexes dashed through into the kitchen, and Worrell and Pryor blasted them back.

"Stay here, keep an eye on her," the Kid ordered, and ran through into the darkened store.

Purcell and two of his clerks were down behind the counters, fighting it out with a bunch of men who were all around the big room, shooting at them. Behind a cracker barrel, Sorreltop Vance bobbed up to fire. The Kid glimpsed the red shaggy hair in the gunflash.

Pryor crouched by the end of the counter. Fast and furious the Colts of the Rio Kid, accurate as Fate, found a shoulder here, a Stetson there. He tried for Vance, evidently spattered splinters and dirt into the redhead's eyes. Sorreltop scuttled out the open front door, cursing and screaming.

His men didn't like the Rio Kid's enfilading fire. Several fell dead as they ran from the store, caught by Purcell and his men. Leaping on their horses, the survivors galloped off into the darkness.

Pryor, out on the porch, helped them on their way with long shots. When they were gone, he pouched his hot guns and turned to see how Conchita was.

"Thanks, Rio Kid," gasped Purcell. "They surprised me this time, but they won't again. From now on I'm keepin' a guard here."

Purcell's foot struck something. He stooped, picked up a black heart carved from cowhide.

"The Black Heart!" he cried.

Startled and afraid, though unhurt, Conchita clung to Worrell.

A couple of hours later, Sheriff Carr's

85

posse rode back into town. They had lost the rustlers' trail in the maze of brush. There had been nothing to do but come home.

The men of Smithville, the Rio Kid quickly found, hardly dared go to work for fear of coming home and finding a loved one stabbed, a symbolic black heart by his or her side. And in the vast, wild jungle of chapparal, almost impenetrable save for the narrow, winding animal trails and a few roads, lurked the cattle thieves.

Sheriffs such as Dave Carr couldn't muster enough men to fight the hordes from across the Rio. Any movements of soldiers or civilian posses were immediately reported by spies. The Army could not cross the Border because of international law.

Pryor and Worrell slept most of the following day in the shack behind the store. In the late afternoon, they dressed and went to the kitchen where Conchita Purcell smilingly fed them a huge meal.

"Reckon I'll go have a look-see 'round yore town," the Rio Kid remarked, knowing that Dan and his girl would appreciate being left alone for awhile.

He strolled down the wooden walk, under the sun awnings. He looked in at the big bar, joined a couple of Sheriff Carr's deputies. They stood each other drinks for an hour, talking over the latest excitement in heated tones.

Always restless, the Rio Kid took leave of them and walked around the plaza. He stopped in a cantina occupied by Mexicans. It had a dirt floor, narrow windows, and the lamps were old and smoky. The men were drinking *tequila,* a fiery liquid distilled from the leaves of the mescal plant. Dark, suspicious eyes fixed upon the *gringo.* The Kid had a drink and looked them over. He had seen plenty of such poor people. They were thick along the Border. He wondered how many might be spies for the cattle thieves across the Rio.

After awhile he went out into the night, glad to breathe in some fresh air after the close atmosphere of the cantina.

The jail and sheriff's office were dark. There was a light on in Purcell's store and more showing in the back rooms where George and his daughter made their home. Smithville appeared to offer little excitement.

"I'd as soon not be stuck here the rest of my born days," he mused.

But his busy mind was figuring ways to come into contact with the gang terrorizing the land. He meant to go after them. He saw some people heading home to bed, the dark figures passing by lighted doorways. Across the chaparral the thin wind moaned, stirring the dry pods of the mesquite, rustling the leaves.

"If I had a hunch where to begin," he muttered, "I'd start huntin' that Black Heart killer. If I could git my hands on Sorreltop Vance for a few minutes, I'd soon find out. Mireles ought to pick up something across the Rio."

He sat in the shadows for awhile, smoking, relaxing from the strenuous events of the ride down from Ellsworth, Kansas, during which he had run into Belle's nest of trouble.

Stars blinked like diamonds overhead. The moon was pushing up over the silver ribbon of the creek that wandered through the brush toward the Rio Grande.

After a time the Kid yawned and stretched, getting up to return to Purcell's.

His rising was suddenly accelerated by a woman's scream. He raced toward the cry that had come from across the plaza.

Bob Pryor saw a lamp come up in the rear of an adobe home near the plaza.

Now the woman screamed in full voice, and other citizens were answering her plea. Bob Pryor turned toward the Mexican house, meaning to hurry inside to give aid. He glimpsed a dark figure, bent low, that scurried from a side door and ran toward the back alley.

"Huh," he grunted.

He swung that way, without hesitation plunging into the inky blackness of the narrow aisle.

He ran full-tilt past the newly lighted windows. The woman was still crying out. Answering yells kept coming from the cantinas. Alert for new alarms, Smithville now was always ready for trouble.

He hit the yard opening behind the house, caught a flash of the man hurrying north along Tin Can Alley. It was impossible to make out any details about the vague figure in the dense shadows cast by the buildings. He started up the alley, drawing a pistol and shouting.

"Hey, stop there! I'm the law, here to help yuh —"

The hombre leaped for a dark doorway, he turned to look back at the Kid. The face was a black masked blob.

A bullet tore within inches of the Rio Kid. He answered once, heard his own hit the thick adobe wall with a dull thud. Then the hombre was gone.

Hustling to the turn-off, he went along

the dark space between homes, toward the lighted street. The plaza seemed filled with scurrying, excited citizens, rushing to answer the wail of the Mexican woman.

"Who the hell's that? What yuh totin' that gun for?"

The Kid, hunting for the man he was chasing, was roughly seized by a couple of big hombres who came from the groups on the plaza. None too gently he was turned toward the light.

"Why, it's the Kid! What's up? Yuh see anything?"

The two were a pair of Carr's deputies who had ridden on the fruitless chase to Belle's hideout at Hell's Gate. They released him, but by that time there was no following the fugitive. Whoever it had been had made good his escape.

After hunting up and down for a few minutes, Pryor went back to the Mexican adobe. There be found a peon woman dissolved in tears over the body of her nephew, for whom she had kept house. The slim young Mexican-American had been stabbed to the heart. The knife had been withdrawn, and he had bled profusely.

At his side Bob Pryor saw the six-inch black heart cut from cured cowhide.

Sheriff Dave Carr came hurrying up, his

bearded face grave. Immediately he took charge and a crowd collected inside and out. At Pryor's suggestion, Carr obtained a lantern and they went around back to search for footprints.

The ground was baked hard and held few imprints, but the sheriff discovered a boot-mark in a bit of sandy dirt near the house corner. A high heel of the type worn by riders, it was common in the southwest. The sole was curved and narrow, but Pryor quickly pointed out that it was one of his own, left when he had chased the assassin. They went on until the Rio Kid, bent with eyes close to the ground, indicated a flat, shapeless mark that seemed fresh.

"He wore moccasins," he observed.

But the track was lost in the beaten ground around the livery stable where the Kid had left Saber. The dun, scenting his beloved master, whinnied and came galloping up to the fence of the corral, which ran some distance behind the stable. There were other horses in there as well and Saber had made himself king of the lot with his domineering temper. Saddles hung on the top fence rail, Pryor's among them.

Large crowds of citizens, Mexicans and Texans had come forth. The saloons were emptied, and men appeared in jackets and boots pulled on over their sleeping garments. Excited talk rose in the cool air of the night.

For half an hour Sheriff Carr looked about. Whoever had done the stabbing had escaped in the night.

Terror again had come upon Smithville. Citizens stared into the dark shadows. Superstitious fear gripped the population. The Black Heart murderers had chosen the exact course of scaring them with this ugly symbolism. More than one Mexican spoke of packing up and getting out of town in a hurry.

For a time Bob Pryor poked around back alleys, hunting further signs of the assassin. Sheriff Carr saddled up, and with several deputies, started out to ride a circle about the settlement to make sure there were no bands of masked killers lurking, ready to pounce, as had happened when Sorreltop Vance attacked the general store. Also, the officer hoped that perhaps he might hit on some trace of the murderer.

Pryor finally went back to the shack behind George Purcell's. Dan Worrell came out of the kitchen where he had been sitting with Conchita.

"Shore terrible," growled Worrell, as they pulled off their boots, hung up their Stetsons and made ready to retire. "I don't savvy what the killer aims at doin', Bob. He seems to be wipin' out sev'ral families of folks in these parts. But why?"

The Kid shrugged. "We need someone to talk. Someone like Vance, for instance. Then we'll know. It's a cinch whoever's doin' it ain't doin' it for fun. He's takin' a good many chances. And if he gits caught near here, I'd say Judge Lynch would operate mighty fast!"

"Yuh're right there. I don't b'lieve anybody, not even Carr, could hold off these folks if they ever was convinced they had the feller doin' these murders."

"When it's light, I'm goin' to start on Vance's trail," Pryor said.

Worrell blew out the candle and got into the hard bunk across the cabin from Bob Pryor. The two young fellows quickly fell asleep. Their nerves were in splendid condition and the bracing air and physical life they led made sleep easy for them. . . .

The Rio Kid awoke with a start, instantly in full command of all his faculties. He had the trained sensitivity of an Indian, due to his army training as a scout and to years on the Frontier. A man survived or died, depending on his ability to act fast in time of trouble.

Pryor's weapons, and the two he toted under his shirt, hung from the back of a chair, close to his hand while he slept.

He heard Worrel's bunk creaking as the young giant shifted to an alert sitting position.

"Dan — Dan, quick!" The woman's excited whisper came to them from the door.

"What's wrong, Conchita?" Worrell demanded, jumping to the portal, picking up a double-barreled shotgun that stood close at hand.

The Kid sat up, pulling on his boots. As Worrell opened the door, he could see the girl's slight figure in the cold moonlight outside. And, in the background, he heard a familiar growing sound, vague yet menacing. He could make out the growling of many voices that joined together in a chorus.

"A mob," he whispered. "Wonder where they're headin' —"

"Quick, Dan, tell Bob to run for it," Conchita gasped hurriedly. "They're coming here to lynch him! Hurry!"

"What?" gasped Worrell. "Why — What —"

"Don't stop to talk," she begged, looking fearfully over her slim shoulder, covered by a silk wrap. "They're excited. They'll hang

94

him first and talk afterward. Oh, Bob — Go on, run, get a horse and ride —"

Chapter IX
Lynch Mob

Lithe as a panther in his movements, the Rio Kid buckled on his gun-belt, stuck the shoulder holsters in place. His pockets were crammed with fresh shells when he sprang to the door. Worrell reached out to hold him back. Infuriated men could already be seen rapidly approaching the shack.

"There he ees! Drag heem out!"

"Git outa the way, Conchita," a Texan roared.

Shots were fired into the air. They did not wish to harm the young woman.

"Hustle back into the store, Conchita." He was afraid she would get hurt in the swiftly approaching riot.

"What're they after me for?" Pryor asked emotionlessly.

"Damn if I know," Worrell replied in bewilderment.

But neither was the kind to run from danger. The huge young Texan held a double-barreled shotgun as he faced the oncoming mob. Most of them were Mexicans, but leading them were a couple of Sheriff Carr's possemen, citizens who were sworn in when a hunt was up. Several of the men in front had lariats looped up and hanging from their arms.

Furious curses were flung at the slim Rio Kid, who took his stand beside Worrell. Dan reached out and forced Conchita back inside the cabin, out of harm's way. A bullet shrieked over their heads, but they stood their ground.

Faster and faster came the mob, urged on by those in back.

"What's wrong? What's the idee?" Worrell began yelling.

The Kid stood, arms akimbo, hands close to his shoulder holsters, curiously watching the approach of ignominious death at the hands of a lynch mob.

Dan Worrell elevated the double-barreled shotgun.

"Stand where yuh be," he snarled.

"Put down zat gun! Take eet away! Leench heem!"

Those in back pushed the men in front, shoving them almost into Worrell's gun. The leaders, faced by the steady muzzles, stopped in their tracks and leaned back hard.

"Hey, Dan, yuh wouldn't shoot an old pard," one of the erstwhile deputies growled. He was not a regular officer but an honest citizen, sometimes working as a cowhand, at other times as a store clerk.

"I'll pull these triggers, hell or high water," yelled Dan, " 'less yuh tell me what's up."

To the Kid's surprise, knowing mobs as he did, the deputy was willing to parley. "Fetch the evidence," he ordered.

A man came from the crowd, carrying a saddle. Two more brought burning pitch torches, which gave a hellish glow to the scene.

Alert, Worrell and the Rio Kid stood with their backs to the shack wall. The hombre dumped the saddle on the ground a few feet in front of them and then backed away from the shotgun.

The deputy, a cavernous-faced, thin fellow, pointed down.

"Whose saddle is this?" he demanded.

"Mine," drawled the Kid.

"What I tal' you," a shrill-voiced Mexican cried. The Kid recognized the wrangler of the livery stable where he had left Saber. "*Si*, I wak' up at loud noise. I see an hombre snik from ze saddle. He throw knife my way, I go out, fin' eet fall to groun'. Zen I look and fin' all zat!"

98

Instantly Bob Pryor realized that he had been planted. He began figuring on getting away from there. He knew that a lynch mob does not think. While the units making it up might be decent, kindly folks alone, in aggregate they are motivated by herd savagery.

The Mex wrangler was young. He might have been purposely roused and drawn out to find the evidence.

Growls of hate rose from the throats of the citizens. The Rio Kid was a stranger, and the proof had more than convinced them.

The deputy squatted down. He opened one of the saddle pocket snaps, and drew forth a piece of what the Kid saw was cowhide. He held it high, so Worrell and the crowd could see. From the center had been cut a rough heart-shaped chunk.

"Here y'are," he yelled. "I got the black heart that was left by Espinosa's body las' evenin'." Holding both above his head, he forced the heart into the hide. It fitted perfectly, all the irregularities of the heart dovetailing into the opening.

"And if that ain't enough," he crowed, "look at this!" From the other leather pouch of the Rio Kid's saddle, he extracted a dark cloth. He unwrapped this and inside lay a long bowie knife. "Blood still on the blade, though he wiped most of it off! Yuh're purty clever, Mister Rio Kid, but seems to me yuh knowed an awful lot 'bout the Black Heart business! Yuh got us way up to Hell's Gate on a wild-goose chase, and yuh tried to lay it on Sorreltop Vance. Mebbe Vance is in cahoots with yuh. He'll git the same treatment we mean to give you."

"Stand back, damn yuh," gasped Worrell. Confused by the terrible proof showed him, he glanced quickly at the Rio Kid. "Bob," he muttered. "I — I can't savvy —"

The Rio Kid, eyes on the leaders, a smile touching his good-humored mouth, faced the crowd.

"Yuh're barkin' up the wrong tree, boys. Somebody planted them things in my pouches. I kin prove to yuh I had nuthin' to do —"

"Shut heem up!" shrieked an excited, impatient Mexican.

"Streeng heem to ze neares' tree. Don' leesten to hees lies!"

With a roar the mob surged forward. They would not hear what they would not believe.

A horseman came galloping full-tilt past Purcell's store and cut into the crowd, quirting folks out of his path, roaring at them to desist. It was Sheriff Dave Carr.

"What the hell's all this?" he bawled, flinging himself off leather. "What's this mob doin' here?"

A dozen hands reached out to seize the protesting, angry sheriff.

"Go 'way, don't try to stop this," snapped the leading deputy.

"Now look, Lew," Carr said, "I can't have no lynchin' in my town."

"Dry up!"

"Go chase yoreself, Sheriff!"

"He's guilty as hell," Lew told Carr. "It's proved to the hilt, Dave. That Rio Kid feller stabbed Espinosa tonight and in his pack we found the knife and the chunk of hide the black heart was cut from! Mebbe he seemed to fight for Purcell, but it must've been a blind to work in with us."

"I don't care if he's guilty of ev'ry dang murder in Texas!" Carr roared. "He's my pris'ner now and yuh can't take him. C'mon, Pryor."

"I'll go with the sheriff," the Kid said lazily.

"Like hell yuh will!"

The scant patience of the lynch mob was exhausted. Fury broke on the air about the shack. Carr, held powerless, could only struggle futilely in the hands of his captors.

Bob Pryor had no desire to injure these citizens. Misguided though they were, he would not fight them. But Worrell let go with one barrel of the shotgun, close over the heads of the leaders. The rush hesitated.

"Next time I fire lower," shouted Worrell.

The Rio Kid suddenly jumped back, through the open door of the shack. In the wall of the other side was an open window and he leaped through it, hitting the shadowed ground on the other side. The men in front surged around Dan Worrell, snatching the shotgun from his hands. For a moment or two, which gave Pryor time to get started, the huge young Texan beat them off with his fists, blocking the doorway. Then they were inside.

"There he goes, out the winder!" shrieked a sharp-eyed hombre who had glimpsed the Kid dashing away from the hut.

Immediately they turned, splitting around the shack as a wave separates around a rock. The Rio Kid almost made the shelter of the wall on the far side of the store. As he lunged for it, he was framed for a second against the yellow light shaft from the kitchen window. A fusillade of bullets ripped at him. He ran into one, felt the sickening stab as it hit high up on his thigh. It burned like a red-hot iron, paralyzing his left leg. He fell, rolling head over heels out of sight behind the store.

Howls of triumph went up.

Pulling himself together after the shock, the Kid got to his feet almost instantly. He ran, limping, on to the front, where stood a number of animals, left there by members of the mob. A couple of bullets, sent from swift-footed hombres who were first to the alley, sang close behind him. Always as an accompaniment came the noise of the mob, the growling, confused hum of a swarm of giant bees.

Fighting back the pain in his leg, the Kid mounted the nearest horse. Then he deliberately kicked out on all sides with his spurred boot heels, breaking the whole line into a confused mass, to delay pursuit. He bent low over the animal and rode hell-for-leather across the plaza, seeking to get behind the jail walls for cover in his escape. The chaparral was not far off. Once in it, he figured he would be safe.

Most of the mob followed directly in his wake, up the opening where he had fallen. But several shrewder men came through the other side and made a few seconds on the escaping victim of their blind fury. It was one of these who took steady aim and hit the Kid's horse. The animal faltered in his stride, but then drove on.

"How bad yuh hurt, boy?" whispered the

Kid anxiously. He could not stop to find out. Looking back, he saw that some animals had been caught and mounted. He had to reach the bush before they came close.

He took the first trail through the dense, thorned chaparral, urging on the horse he had borrowed. The animal was gasping hard with agony, but kept going. The hue and cry of frantic pursuit tore after them.

The Kid hit the creek crossing. Belly deep the horse waded through and broke into the brush on the west side.

"Wish I had Saber under me," he muttered. Behind him he could see waving red torch flares as the rest of the men mounted and started after him.

To escape without injuring any citizens was the Rio Kid's object. He might have used his guns to hold them off, but it would have meant putting lead into innocent folks who had been misled by some hidden, slimy enemy.

"He's the one I'll git," the Kid promised himself.

The horse was a trained brush-popper, skilful in weaving in and out of the narrow cattle and deer trails made in the chaparral. Several times the Kid was nearly swept from his back by hanging limbs, but he kept low, clinging to mane and horn. Long, stilettolike thorns tore at his flesh.

Suddenly the animal gave a convulsive leap which nearly threw the Kid from his seat. Pryor managed to get his toes out of the tap-covered stirrups just in time. He landed in a bush as the horse crashed dead beneath him.

He picked himself up, looked back toward his pursuers. They were hunting him, a difficult feat in the darkness of the dense chaparral, despite their torches. It would take daylight to do any fast tracking in these hoof-beaten, narrow mazes of trails. Now that his horse was gone, he must depend on cunning to make good his escape.

His mind, cool in this moment of peril, harked back to the Civil War. Once he had had a horse shot under him by a Confederate picket, and had escaped only by taking to a river near at hand. All his training instantly urged him to make for the creek. The water would hide his tracks, and it would give him a clear avenue along which to wade. The horsemen would be some time getting around to his foot-trail.

He doubled back, then, toward the water, nearer to the town. To the north of him the torch lights told him just where his enemies were. Slowly they were working south. He was at the bank of the creek when he heard a man call out at the top of his voice.

"Hey, boys, here's his horse, shot dead!"

"We've got him now," crowed another.

Pryor slid into the water, started wading as fast as he could in the shallows.

The shooting pains in his leg increased. Each movement cost him dearly. But he gritted his teeth and continued. Knowing the ways of trackers, the Kid stuck to the creek. Reeds grew in thick patches here and there. He could hide in them if necessary.

But his leg kept getting worse. The wound was rapidly sapping his power. Soaking wet, disheveled, the Rio Kid kept his head. As yet he was not far from the town. By turning, he could see the yellow glow of Smithville. Chaparral grew dense among the higher trees fringing the creek. He doggedly shoved on but at last he knew he had to stop. His leg would carry him no farther. He was so close to collapse that he had to start hunting a place to hide.

He picked a spot where the widening creek seemed to have an undercut bank that was toward the settlement. He had left no trail that could be found by the expert sign-followers who would get to work in the morning.

CHAPTER X
WAY OF THE RANGERS

A tinge of dawn touched the sky behind the town. Worn to a frazzle and badly wounded, the Rio Kid worked his body in under the clay bank. Still in the water, he found he could go several yards along a strange stone-lined passage from the stream.

Hunting a dry spot where he might lie, he proceeded for some distance before he came to a place where caved-in rocks blocked him. There he was able to get up on the side and lie, panting for breath.

The trackers, good as they were, would have a hard time locating him now. When he was rested and feeling stronger, he could steal out. In the darkness of the next night, he might get another horse, perhaps even call Saber from the corral behind the livery stable.

He lay in the damp air of the inlet. The blackness was so pitch that he could not see his own hand held before his eyes. Dankness bit at his wound, yet, far in as he had crept, the air was good. It seemed almost draughty as it blew past him.

After awhile he overcame the pain in his leg and fell into a feverish half sleep from which he was startled. Dimly he heard thudding steps over him, not far away, and then men's voices. They were hunting him. A blotch of brownish light faintly illuminated the mouth of the hole into which he had crept.

Then he slept again. The hunters had passed on, cursing, bewildered by the mysterious disappearance of their quarry. . . .

When he woke up, he felt weak, and his lips were dry and cracked. He pulled himself over far enough to scoop up a hatful of water, drank his fill, bathed his face. He did not know how long he had slept.

He was not hungry, though he knew his belly must be sticking to his backbone. Only by a supreme effort of his strong will was he able to roll into the shallow inlet. He began to crawl and rest, crawl and rest, till he finally came to the outer air.

It was dusk, though the afternoon warmth still hung over the dusty chaparral. By the help of a tree trunk he pulled himself erect and tried out his wounded leg. It was stiff and agonizing, but it held him. He wiped the water from his eyes, looking about him. Birds trilled in the trees. A mule-eared rabbit stared, surprised, at the strange creature which had emerged from the undercut bank of the creek.

"Don't worry," the Kid muttered. "I don't aim to eat rabbit stew tonight!"

He got up into the bush, found a cattle trail and worked toward Smithville. The bush was extremely dense here. He had to skirt several grass-covered, strange mounds. Once he stubbed against a massive, round stone, its concave top filled with dirt.

When he reached the edge of the brush, he lay down and rested, waiting for the enveloping cloak of the night. The town, he could see from where he lay, was quiet enough.

"Wonder how long I lay up in there," he muttered.

He felt his chin. His beard was bristly with a two or three day growth. And he had been clean-shaven the night he escaped from the lynch mob! Feverish nightmare had devoured those missing hours.

Patience was a major part of his shrewd scouting instinct. He did not rush out at the fall of the darkness. It was along toward ten o'clock before the stealthy, dark figure left the shelter of the chaparral. He crept from bit of cover to bit of cover, a tree here, a bush there, and then a rock, toward Smithville.

He came up to the corral fence behind the livery stable. There was a light on in the building. He kept the fence between himself and the stable while he strained his eyes in the darkness for signs of Saber. Horse shapes stood in the corral and the wind puffed against the Kid's drying back.

He gave a faint whistle, heard an answering whinny. Up came the dun, rested and well fed, nuzzling through the wooden fence bars. Pryor began to remove a section. They fitted tightly but he got a couple down. He walked the horse to the front, and picked a saddle off the top rail.

The click-click of a cocking rifle stopped him. The young Mexican wrangler stepped from the shadows. "So, Senor Keed. You come back. I theenk you would. I watch!"

"Who told yuh to say that was my stuff in the bags, muchacho?" growled Pryor, staring at the rifle muzzle.

"Who? No one. I see you snik up, *si*. Deesmount, I tak' you to ze shereef."

"Okay," the Kid replied. He suddenly flung the saddle at the wrangler, knocked him over. He leaped, landed on top of the

110

Mexican, and ripped the rifle away. Holding him by the throat, cutting off his cries, he snarled, "Tell the truth, boy. Who's yore chief in this? Yuh planted them things in my saddle-bags."

"No, Senor, no —"

He convinced himself this lad was innocent. Whoever had put the knife and cowhide in the bags had fooled the wrangler, a simple tool.

"Cinch on that saddle," he ordered, and the scared wrangler obeyed.

Shadowy forms appeared, hurrying around the stable. Someone called out.

"What's goin' on back here?"

The Mex youth, with a strangled cry, fell flat on his face. The Rio Kid whirled the dun and flashed along the corral fence.

Explosions hurriedly fired after the fugitive rang in the night. Evidently others had also been watching the livery stable in case the Kid returned. He heard the close whine of bullets, but the dun, zigzagging, sped away unhindered.

Pursuit began but it was futile. No horse could overtake Saber. The Kid forded the creek and galloped up the trail out of the valley, soon losing them.

As he topped the ridge, he looked back, face a steely mask.

"Yuh'll see me again," he muttered.

He pushed on for several miles, southwest toward the Rio Grande, and finally pulled up in thick chaparral. He chewed some hardtack biscuits he found in one of the pouches of the borrowed saddle. But he wanted fresh meat, which would give him strength.

About him were cracklings in the brush, wild cattle and deer, javelinas, the wild pig of the chaparral, hunting food and water. They slept throughout the day and did their feeding and drinking at night.

Luck was with him and knowledge of such tricks. Hearing a number of animals that sounded too slight for cows, he decided it must be a herd of the small deer. These little animals had accommodated their bodies to fit the stunted jungles of the chaparral.

He dismounted and took out his waterproof matchbox. He broke off a dry branch, which he set afire. It blazed up blindingly bright. The deer ran off, but fatal curiosity brought them back to stare at the light. He raised his Colt and fired.

Half an hour later he had a blaze going, and the skinned haunch of a deer sent forth an appetizing aroma.

He slept a mile away from the location of

his fire, a usual precaution in hostile country.

The best parts of the cooked deer meat he wrapped in clean leaves and packed in the saddle-bags. Then the Rio Kid found a little rill of water and cleaned up as best he could, but he was unable to shave. His leg was healing, for there was no infection, despite the experience he had undergone.

The sun rose and the warmth flowed into his body. Though still lame, he was quickly regaining his strength.

He rode south for the Rio Grande. Over there lay Las Cuevas, where his friend Mireles had gone.

"Reckon I'll run into to him sooner or later if I watch the ford," he thought. "I got to git goin' on Vance and his chief's trail!"

He followed a faint cattle trace, keeping off the main way to the ford. Here the Rio was so deep that it was necessary to swim to reach old Mexico.

Alert as ever, in the afternoon the dun gave him a warning, rippling his black stripe. The Kid was immediately on guard.

He slipped from Saber's back. Hand on gun, he tiptoed to the turn in the trail ahead. Peering through the interstices of bush, Pryor saw a sleepy looking paint horse standing, saddle on its back. No rider was in sight.

A chuckle close behind him caused him to stiffen. He started to whirl, but the click of a rifle trigger told him he had stepped into a clever trap.

"Ah ha," a mellow Mexican voice cried. "You walk right up, Senor! Drop ze guns. Put up ze han's, pronto!" There was a hard note to the last word, and the Kid was not fooled by the laughter of his captor.

Slowly, hands up, he turned. Staring at him from a thick bush where he had cunningly hidden himself, leaving his horse around the bend as a bait, was a chunky, middle-aged Mexican with a seamed face and great handlebar mustache.

"Who are you, Senor?" asked the man softly.

The Kid had believed the disreputable looking Mexican to be a spy, perhaps one of Xavier Gonzales' own band. But, taking in the shrewd old eyes, the way the fellow handled himself, he was not so sure of this. The man might be a good citizen. On the other hand he could be one of the hundreds of peons who worked for the Mexican thieves.

"Why stick a gun on me, *caballero?*" drawled Pryor, seeking for some hint of how to address his captor.

"Hah. You weesh to know? You ask? Why you snik up like zat Senor-weeth-no-shave? You try to catch old Casuse but — ha-hah — old Casuse catch you!" He roared with merriment at the grim jest.

"Jest takin' the usual precaution, Senor Casuse," the Kid said smoothly.

Bob Pryor tried to edge a bit closer, within striking distance. But Jesus Sandoval was too foxy to be fooled by such a trick. It was ten years since Casuse, as his name had been twisted by the Texans, had slept in his own house near the Rio Grande. He had hanged several Mexican bravos he had caught stealing his cattle, and their numerous relatives had sworn vengeance. Casuse always slept in the chaparral a mile or two from home and never twice in the same spot.

"Keep back, keep back," said Casuse cheerfully, gun always aimed at Pryor's vitals. "Mebbe, Senor, you do not lik' ze law? Eef so, I know mannee lik' you."

It seemed a hint.

"Mebbe not, Casuse. Which is one reason I like to see who's ahead of me on a trail!"

"*Bueno*, lots of ze boys are on ze dodge. Try to join my *amigo*, General Juan Flores, *si?*"

"A good idee."

Casuse laughed till tears rolled down his seamed cheeks.

"Come, we can't stan' here to talk all day. Mount, Senor, mount."

He whistled and the old paint horse lazily plodded up.

"Kin I call my horse now?" asked the Kid casually.

"*Si, si.* But of course."

Pryor whistled to the dun. But instead of Saber's favorite tune, "Said the Big Black Charger," the Kid shrilled several bars of the cavalry "Charge."

Nostrils widening, snorting, the fighting dun galloped in. He went right into action, biting and kicking at the surprised paint horse, who only tried to get out of the angry dun's reach. In the uproar, the paint horse bumped Casuse and knocked him back into a thorn bush. Howling, the Mexican leaped out, found himself staring into the Kid's leveled pistol.

"Now," drawled Pryor, "tables're turned, Casuse. S'pose yuh do a little song and dance for me."

Casuse shrugged. He could read the stern eyes of the Kid. The way Pryor handled his Colt impressed him.

A sudden crackle of brush sent Pryor jumping behind his prisoner. Two young men, toting .50 caliber needle guns and Colt .45s, wearing brown Stetsons and well mounted, shoved in.

"What the hell's wrong, Casuse?" demanded one.

"Hey, Callicott! Thees bandeet hav' me!"

The Rio Kid saw they were Texans of his own brand, young fighting men.

"Drop yore gun, hombre," ordered the stalwart youth Casuse had addressed as Callicott.

"Go on, shoot! Shoot through me, I don't care," Casuse shouted.

But they would not hurt their Mexican friend.

"Who are yuh?" demanded Pryor. "Yuh're shore not friends of the rustlers."

"No, we ain't," replied Callicott. "We're Cap'n McNelly's men. Yuh better put up that gun."

"I will," the Kid promised, "if yuh'll take me to McNelly, boys."

"That's jest what we aim to do."

Pryor let his Colt slide back into the supple holsters. He turned his back on them, deliberately, and mounted.

"Ride on ahead," Bill Callicott said. "It ain't far."

CHAPTER XI
ATTACK ON RANGERS

Single file, they rode a winding trail through the brush for two miles. They came to a small clearing set around a little spring in the marshes. About fifteen men of the same stamp as Callicott were lounging around, resting, washing clothes, cooking up beef and mutton, polishing guns and equipment.

A tall, slim gentleman with an intellectual's high brow, clear, gentle blue eyes, a pointed mustache under which was a round beard, rose from the shade of a gnarled oak and stepped over to them. He wore dark riding clothes and a straight, black Stetson.

"Who is this?" he asked, his voice very soft, with a caressing drawl. His whole manner seemed that of a timid preacher.

"We come on this hombre," Callicott reported. "He had old Casuse under his gun but he rode along with us. Didn't put up no fight, Captain."

"No savvy heem," shrugged Jesus Sandoval. "He on ze dodge, *Capitan.*"

The Rio Kid got down from his horse, saluted snappily.

"Captain McNelly, I'm happy to meet yuh, sir. I've heard plenty of yuh. My name's Bob Pryor. They call me the Rio Kid."

A troubled line deepened in the high, smooth forehead of the great Texas Ranger.

"This is very strange," McNelly remarked in his gentle way. "Why, sir, you were not captured by my men, but rode here willingly?"

"Yes, Captain," the Kid said. "What's wrong?"

McNelly shook his head sadly. A judge of men, he could see through Pryor's dirt stains and beard stubble.

"You know why I'm down here, Mr. Pryor. My purpose is stoppin' the rustlin', murderin' and burnin's. Nothin's goin' to stop us from haltin' those Mexicans of General Flores. But I've heard of you, sir — heard you're a first-rate fightin' man. Too bad, because I've got the lists of wanted criminals in this county. Sheriff Carr of Smithville wants you for murder. And it's my duty to turn you in, though I shore wish you could'a been on our side, sir."

"That's an error, Captain," the Kid replied. McNelly's bravery, his exploits as a law officer, recommended him to Bob Pryor. He wanted to be friendly with McNelly, help him if possible.

McNelly cleared his throat, looked down at his elegant boots.

"With so few men it is impossible for me to take prisoners. And yet, if I release those captured by us, they will give warning to their friends."

A diversion was created as two Rangers rode in with a Mexican prisoner they had captured in the brush. He was a stocky, scowling hombre, with close-set eyes and a fierce appearance.

"Ha, ees Telesforo Jimines," cried Casuse.

"You know him, Casuse?" inquired McNelly.

"*Si, si!* Ees one of Gonzales' spies." He lapsed into rapid Spanish, to which Jimines refused to reply. Casuse immediately brought up his paint horse and ordered Jimines aboard, after roping the spy's hands behind him and dropping a noose around the criminal's neck.

Pryor watched. Casuse seemed most expert at this. He tossed the end of the rope over a tree limb and yanked the spy up and down a few times. Then he again questioned Jimines, who gave some information.

"He say he know notheeng, *Capitan*. He hav' been up north, to steal plenty cattle, and ees on way to Las Cuevas."

The Ranger leader's eyes were somber. He nodded, turned away.

"Queer," the Kid heard him mutter, "no activity since I've got here. Now I wonder —" He broke off. Chin on breast, hands folded at his back, he stood immersed in thought.

The Rio Kid watched as Casuse led the paint horse a short way from camp, supposedly out of sight, although the Kid could plainly see what went on. The Mexican guide for McNelly tossed the lariat end over the limb of a tree, whistling a carefree tune as he worked. Then he hit the old paint horse a terrific lick with his belt. The animal jumped mightily, leaving the spy dangling with a broken neck. Casuse mounted and rode back to camp.

Evidently McNelly did not like this method of disposing of criminals. But Bob Pryor, knowing what military necessity demanded, realized it was the only way for McNelly to achieve his purpose. He did not have enough men to keep prisoners, and if he turned them loose they would rouse all the owlhooters.

"Suppose," McNelly said to Pryor, "you

have something to eat and drink, sir."

"Thanks, Captain."

Beef, bread, coffee and whiskey were passed to the visitor. The Kid stuffed himself and rolled a cigarette. After smoking, he borrowed a razor and a cake of soap from Bill Callicott. Going to the spring, he spruced up till he looked himself again.

"I have thought this matter over carefully," Captain McNelly announced. "I have reached this conclusion, sir. Not only Sheriff Carr wants you, Pryor. The whole town of Smithville claims you are guilty of a terrible murder, something concerning a black heart cut from cowhide. There seems to be a number of these killings unsolved. You can hardly expect me to let you go free. On the other hand, I can't spare men to watch you."

"Well, Captain," drawled the Rio Kid, a smile on his lips and his eyes careless with humor. "You can't expect me to mount old Casuse's paint horse the way that Mexican spy did. I told yuh there was a mistake. I'm the man wanted in Smithville, but I was planted." Quickly he told McNelly of the lynch mob, the evidence against himself, and of his escape.

The captain shook his head sadly. "I am an officer of the State of Texas, Pryor. It's my duty to turn in persons wanted by the law — that is, if I can do so," he added, with a glance back at the spot where the Mexican had been hung. "In deference to you, I'll consider this. Instead of taking care of you myself, I'll send you back to Smithville under guard and turn you over to the sheriff."

"Yuh better hang me yoreself," remarked the Kid dryly. "It would save lots of trouble, Captain. Those folks'll bust in the jail to take me."

"It's the only way I can think of," McNelly insisted. "After all, your prosecution isn't my affair. It's only a day's run to Smithville, and two of my boys will take you there, whenever you're ready."

"I'm not aimin' on goin' back to Smithville — jest yet, anyway," the Rio Kid said slowly.

The two looked straight into one another's eyes. Both were rugged individualists and unyielding as steel. The Kid had left off his gun-belt, but he had two pistols hidden under his shirt and vest. Neither man would give in. McNelly, believing the charge against Pryor, would order his men to shoot if the Kid attempted to escape. But Pryor would not injure one of the Rangers. Several of McNelly's young fellows, hardened, tanned Texans, unostentatiously picked up their needle guns, ready to carry out their commander's wishes.

"Someone comin', Cap'n," reported Ranger Tom Sullivan.

"It's Lieutenant Robinson," sharp-eyed Callicott said.

A lean man, McNelly's next in command, rode into camp. Behind him came a huge Ranger on a great black stallion. The Rio Kid, after a brief look at the lieutenant, turned to the other man. It was Dan Worrell, his friend from Smithville. Worrell looked stern, unhappy.

"Howdy, Dan," the Kid sang out.

Worrell nearly fell off his horse when he saw the Rio Kid. His face brightened up and he hit the ground. Grabbing the Kid's hand he pumped it.

"Bob! Doggone, I thought yuh was dead! Where in tarnation yuh been hidin'? How'd yuh git away?"

"Crawled into a hole and stayed there," replied Pryor. "So yuh've joined up with Captain McNelly."

"Shore. I'm sort of in disgrace in town. For — Well, never mind that."

"For helpin' me, I s'pose. I couldn't have made it without yore aid, Dan."

Worrell nodded. "Even George Purcell

turned against me, when yuh got away. Though yuh helped save him that night, he finally decided it was a trick. Told me not to come round any more. Oh, Conchita will stick with me through hell and high water, but ev'rybody in Smithville give me the cold-shoulder. I rode out and hooked up with the captain. Figger on gittin' some revenge on Vance and Gonzales and their thieves."

"So Purcell believes I done that murder?"

"Yeah, ev'rybody does. Even Conchita, Bob, though she'll help me in anything. Why, I believe it myself, till yuh face me!"

"That evidence was planted. I reckon whoever's workin' with Sorreltop Vance in Smithville didn't like me comin' as close as I did. After all, you and I showed the law that big hideout they had for a depot."

McNelly was listening interestedly to the conversation.

"What's your opinion on this, my boy?" he asked Worell

"Captain," Dan replied earnestly, "I'd like to tell yuh jest what happened." Quickly he described his first meeting with Pryor, when the Kid had fought Sorreltop Vance, Gonzales, John Wesley Hardin and others at Belle Starr's to rescue him.

"Hardin!" repeated McNelly, and his lips

grew tight. "I'd kill every horse I have to catch that blackguard. When I'm finished down here I'll go after him."

He mused for a time over Dan's story concerning the Rio Kid. At last he spoke.

"All right, sir. It's plain there's been some mistake made. I've heard of yuh before and know you're not an outlaw but a good citizen. Of course you may be guilty of the murder in Smithville. But after what Worrell tells me I find that hard to believe. Obviously you're no friend of the cattle thieves I'm after. I'm goin' to turn you loose. But — keep out of my way, you understand?"

Bob Pryor shrugged, nodded. "It's yore roll, Captain. However, I expect to clear up these Black Heart killin's, if only to clear myself." He shook Worrell's hand, started toward his horse, picking up his guns. McNelly came after him, stuck out his hand. The Kid shook with him.

Swinging into Saber's saddle, Pryor rode west out of the Texas Rangers camp. Dan Worrell was looking after him with an unhappy expression on his square face.

The Rio Kid did not go far. Turning off into the dense chaparral, he made camp and rested himself. He felt better after the shave and washup he had had with the Rangers, though his leg was still stiff. The end of day was close at hand, the sun a tremendous red globe over the Western bush jungle.

He took the saddle off and let Saber roll in the damp grass of the marshlands. Here and there were large areas of shallow pools, grown thick with blood-reeds and weeping willows in great numbers. To the south lay the muddy ribbon of the Rio Grande, deep and wide, and marshes abounded on both sides. Good-sized boats could navigate thus far.

He had been there about an hour. Suddenly, from the direction of the Rangers' camp, he heard the sound of gunfire, and, more dimly, other shots that seemed farther eastward. He climbed a tree near-by, from which he could see back across the stunted jungles. Horsemen were pushing their horses through the winding trails. Those nearer to him he could identify as McNelly and his men. He could hardly make out the opposing force, though he thought they were masked.

The sharp reports of the needle guns and Colts, the heavier booming of Sharps, the whip of Spencer carbines, came to him as he watched the running battle. A large number of men were against McNelly, as the Kid could tell from the smoke-puffs that faced him. But L. H. McNelly never hesitated for such a reason. At the head of his fighting Rangers, Captain McNelly charged, disappearing eastward through the chaparral, hot on the trail of those who had had the temerity to fire on him.

There was a line of puzzlement between the handsome Kid's steely blue eyes.

"Funny way for them rustlers to act," he muttered, as he left the tree, the battle having passed from his sight. "They walk right up to McNelly, whom they're so scairt of!"

Night dropped its velvet, sudden blanket over the vast wilderness of the Rio Grande country. The Kid was ready for more sleep, to recuperate from what he had gone through.

He woke with a start, and the dun was by his side, sniffing at him and snorting.

The moon was up, bathing the chaparral in light. Stars twinkled merrily, and it was clear enough to see a good distance. The Rio Kid stood up, gun in hand.

To the west, and not far off he heard the creak of leather and the bawling of many steers. They were coming south, headed for the Las Cuevas crossing on the Rio Grande!

CHAPTER XII
LAS CUEVAS

From his post in the chaparral, lying flat on a hummock that overlooked the main trail, the Rio Kid spied upon the great cavalcade. Mexican drivers, in serapes and high-peaked sombreros, cigarettes dangling from their lips, were driving a long line of cattle to the crossing. Lieutenants pushed back in the brush, sitting their mustangs as they oversaw the drive. Steers lowed, horned heads bobbing as they charged the one-way trail to Mexico. They would fill the bellies of Cuban soldiers and never see Texas or their rightful owners again.

A flank rider, evidently one of the chiefs, pushed out of line not far from the Kid's hiding-place. He had paused to light up a cigarette, and in the match flare Bob Pryor recognized the evil-faced Sorreltop Vance.

It was hard to hear any sounds over the constant lowing of the beasts, the thud-thud of their heavy hoofs on the sandy dirt. It took a long time for the great herd to pass Pryor's point.

"I savvy," Pryor mused. "Vance and Gonzales had some of their pards fake an attack to draw McNelly away from here so's they could beat him to the river with this stuff!"

There were several hundred mustangs, too, back of the steers, horses stolen from luckless Texas.

Though he had been wounded and kept busy fighting for his life, the Rio Kid's brain had never stopped working. From what he had observed, he believed there was a close connection between these cow thieves and the Black Heart murders which terrorized Smithville.

Everything pointed the direction of the breath of death that was blowing over Texas.

"I shore need to talk with Celestino," he decided. "And I'd like a look at Las Cuevas too."

Few men would have cared to put their heads into such dangerous positions as the Rio Kid did. But his service as a scout during the Civil War, and his later life on the Frontier, had given him a daring possessed by only a handful of the brave.

"If I help McNelly," he decided, "McNelly'll help me."

It was his intention to smash the Black Heart killers, as well as to aid in crushing the cow thieves. He had, besides his desire to assist Texas people, a personal stake in this. First, he wanted to clear his own name of the murder charge against him in Smithville. Again there was Dan Worrell, his friend, who was plainly in danger. And Mireles had come down here to investigate the killings of relatives.

Over the uproar made by the cows and the Mexican drivers, Pryor heard a sharp cry, repeated, from his right. A rider was making his way along the edge, calling out.

"Senor Vance! Senor Vance!"

Sorreltop Vance, about to ride on after lighting his cigarette swung his mustang and started back. Near the Kid's hummock, Vance met the hombre calling to him.

"Hello, Gonzales," he cried. "What's up?"

The Kid strained his ears, heard what Gonzales shouted above the bedlam.

"Pronto, Vance, ze chief weesh to spik to us. He has pris'ner, ees Purcell's *muchacha!* We mus' tak' her weeth us!"

Pryor jumped. Somehow the chief, as Gonzales and Vance called the mysterious devil who egged them on, had captured Conchita Purcell. Fury in his heart against them, he started creeping north. He hoped

131

to glimpse the chief, but he was aware that come what might, he had to rescue the girl.

It was such hard going, with thorns clutching at him, that he was forced toward the trail. Mustangs were galloping by, urged by dusty vaqueros. The Kid, like a shadow, dashed across little open spaces. He dipped into a hollow. Up over the trail he saw a group of men on horses under a giant oak. One, in the center, wore a steeple sombrero and was muffled in a dark cloak, and the others gathered about him.

"There they are," Pryor thought, and sought to get nearer.

The drag of the stolen stock had passed. The trail was empty save for drag dust and a straggler now and then. Blocked by a dense cactus patch, the Kid dared the open way to pass this obstruction between him and the chief. He ran right into a Mexican leading a lame mustang.

The vaquero rounded a turn, walking slowly, trying to save his animal. He wore a sombrero, a curly mustache, a flowing serape. Seeing the Kid he shouted in Spanish.

"Who are you?"

On the knoll, under the oak, a limp bundle of humanity was tied across the saddle of a spare horse. The man in the Mexican hat and enveloping cloak, face a black blob with bandanna mask clear up to the glittering eyes, spoke quickly with his underlings.

"Take her across the Rio and hold her in the village," he ordered, voice gruff and harsh. "This'll force Purcell out. We kin get him and a bunch of his pards when they try to trail her."

"Yuh hear any more 'bout that consarned Rio Kid?" demanded Vance.

The chief spat venomous curses. "Damn him, he came back and got his horse. I figgered he was far away. He didn't show for three days. I had a couple men at the stable but the fools were up front and half asleep at that. He's floatin' round somewhere, and he's got to die. I'll give any man who brings me his scalp a thousand dollars reward. Tell the *jefes*. And don't fergit, McNelly and his Rangers're dangerous medicine. Keep the gangs in Mexico till he's left. We've cleaned up tonight, gittin' this big herd across."

"*Si,* in two days," Gonzales observed, "we start zem to Monterey, when my bravos are rest'."

"*Bueno.* I've got to git back. Purcell'll be huntin' for Conchita. *Adios.*"

On the trail, the Rio Kid, delayed by his

encounter, faced the bravo, replying in liquid Spanish.

"A friend and —" the Kid had begun to say.

Abruptly he was on the Mexican. Since the Kid's getup was that of a Texan, the bravo had for a moment thought him one of the renegades who rode for Vance.

Pryor left the earth, got his man's right arm and throat, drove a knee to the belly as they landed. The lame mustang shied, nearly stepping on them. It limped down the trail. Save for the first startled gasp, the bravo's cries were cut off. He tried to stab the Kid with a leg-sheath knife. Pryor, forced to grip the chicken throat, took a bad clawing.

He snapped the wrist back and let go suddenly. At the same time, he made a snatch for the knife. He got it, and drove it into his opponent. The Mex shuddered. His throat clicked, and he relaxed. It was life or death and the bravo had lost.

The Kid leaped up, dragged the corpse into the mesquite. He darted back and looked toward the knoll. The group had split up.

He ducked just in time to evade Vance and Gonzales as they came along the trail, leading a spare horse with a limp bundle on it.

Close behind them came a half dozen heavily armed bravos. Pryor heard Vance talking.

"The chief's right, Gonzales. No sense tanglin' with McNelly. This big bunch'll keep the business goin' till the Rangers give up. We'll have a clear alley soon to run the stock and the chief'll have what he wants."

"*Si, si —*"

They rode past the Kid.

Stragglers were still coming, men who for some reason couldn't keep up with the gang. The Kid saw no immediate chance of success in trying to save Conchita. She was unconscious, a prisoner, heavily guarded. A scrap would bring an army of bravos against him.

"I'm goin' over," he muttered, and set to work carrying out his daring plan.

He stripped off the dead bravo's clothes and put them on. The pants made a tight fit, giving him a stouter appearance. He donned the jacket, bound the red sash around his middle. Rolling up his own Stetson, he planted the high-peaked sombrero on his head, pulling it well down. Some smears of clay darkened his bronzed face still more. The serape thrown over his shoulders gave him the complete look of a vaquero. He buckled on his guns and the

135

cloak hid them.

Hustling back to Saber, he mounted and pushed out on the still dusty trail. Head down, letting the dun take his own pace, in the moonlight he looked like another Mexican straggler heading home for Las Cuevas. He was near the end of the procession. There were only a few behind him.

As the road neared the Rio Grande, the land became more marshy. Blood-reeds stood high and thick, and willows grew in profusion. The damp odor of the swamps pervaded the air. The road wound in serpentine twists to avoid the worst of the marshes.

Then the Kid saw before him the Rio Grande, silvered by the moonlight. Flowing wide and deep between its banks at this point, it was the boundary between Old Mexico and Texas. The wide bosom of the river was spotted with hundreds of heads, swimming cattle on their one-way trail. The bellowing was terrific. Drivers stood in the shallows on both sides, lashing the beasts into line.

The Kid came up with the busy vaqueros. He saw Sorreltop Vance and Gonzales, off to the side, supervising the crossing.

Shoving in, Pryor began to whip steers with his quirt, now and then screaming a shrill Spanish imprecation. He turned a small bunch of beeves from escaping into the side reeds, pursuing them down the bank into the water.

Saber started swimming, the current of the amber water bearing him down. But there was an opening on the Mexican bank, and Pryor had taken the current into account at the crossing. They landed in the blood-reeds of the shallows. The dun, dripping wet, walked to the sandy shore.

Here all was the same as on the other side — a crush of cursing men and excited, wet beasts. The skilful vaqueros, however, had everything under control. Out of the press in the center emerged a thin stream of steers, heading south on the road to Las Cuevas, three miles inland.

Nobody gave the vaquero on the mud-spattered dun more than a casual glance. He was correct in costume and he worked the cattle like a Mexican herder.

On the flank, Pryor kept working up to the van. Whenever anybody looked his way he was busy with a steer. To the west of them, he gradually eased off, but the chaparral was thick. As they left the river, the underfooting became dry and sandy.

It was not long before he sighted twinkling lanterns ahead. He made for them. They were the lights of a village, surrounded by corrals constructed of crooked poles cut from the stunted jungle growth, and protected by long-thorned brush. A number of hovels, adobe brick with thatched roofs and slanting chimneys, stood inside the corrals.

The Rio Kid neared this Mexican settlement, believing it to be Las Cuevas. But the cattle herd swung past it and went on. He rounded the village and could see, not far before him, the lights of a larger place, a half mile southeast.

Riding on, skirting the thickest chaparral, he finally reached the larger town. It had many more and larger houses, entirely surrounded by palisades, high, sharpened stakes driven deep into the sandy earth. Great corrals stretched for acres about the town, filled with cattle and horses. And the van of the stolen bunch from Texas was being turned into waiting, empty pens.

Lights and the red glow of fires illuminated the whole scene. Hundreds of Mexicans moved around, most of them busy with the new stock. Women, children and oldsters were asleep in the shacks.

"This is it," muttered Pryor.

This was the notorious Las Cuevas, headquarters of the cattle thieves, where they found sanctuary from pursuit.

The odor of frying food, to fill the bellies

of Gonzales' vaqueros, came upon the wind with the chatter of voices and the lowing of the cattle.

The disguised Rio Kid rode the dun to the main gate, which stood open. Seeing several hombres evidently standing guard, he edged away and dismounted, leaving Saber free.

"Wait till yuh hear, savvy?" he told his pet.

Saber would not stray far. He would be ready for the Kid's signal and would come at his master's call. That had saved Pryor's life more than once, and in this town swarming with menace he suspected that Saber's training would again prove its value.

Chapter XIII
Escape

Dust and a confused chorus of shouting herders agitated the air. The Rio Kid, serape wrapped about his lithe body, face stained and shaded by the high Mexican hat, slouched nearer the gate, watching his chance. He intended to get inside and contact Mireles, if possible. If not, he would scout the terrain for McNelly.

Just outside the main gates, surrounded by a number of followers, stood a heavy-set Mexican of middle age. He was smoking a cigarette, and the Kid could see him plainly in the red light of the fires and torches. The man's face was seamed, baked by years of sun. Wearing a thick mustache and fine clothing, he was plainly a person of renown.

"General Juan," one of his friends remarked, "it is a big herd."

"Si, si," replied General Juan, *majordomo* of the town.

Xavier Gonzales came riding from the village. He paused to speak with the *major-domo*. The Kid figured the bravo boss had left Conchita Purcell in one of the shacks.

"They have come on the one-way trail," Gonzales cried. "General Juan Flores, those steers will never tread Texas soil again."

"You have won a great deal, Gonzales," replied Juan Flores Salinas, *majordomo* of Las Cuevas.

The Rio Kid, chin down so his sombrero brim would hide his face, leaned against the gate. He slipped inside the village while everybody was looking at Flores and Gonzales.

Fires burned in stone hearths about him. Mangy dogs, growling, came to sniff suspiciously at him, but newcomers were common enough in Las Cuevas. There were sleeping forms around. Through the open doors of domiciles the Kid could see bedded children and women.

A quick survey showed that the other entrances to the village were small, heavily barred gates. The main way was the best point of attack. His military eye took in the various larger buildings. Some had very thick walls of adobe. The home of General Juan Flores was a substantial cottage with a wide chimney.

Not as yet did he see Celestino Mireles.

Finally he sat down with his back to a shadowed wall, where he could watch the procession at the gates. He would not dare test his Mexican disguise so far as to show himself here after daylight, and dawn was not more than a couple of hours off. In that time he must get Conchita and be on his way back to Texas.

Among a bunch of Mexicans who came in from the corrals, he at last saw Celestino's lean boyish figure slip from the back of a white mustang. He had been working at the pens, and had left off his serape. Since the Kid had seen him in disguise before the lad had left for Las Cuevas, he recognized Mireles quickly.

Celestino went over to the big *olla* and took a long drink. Then he turned off and passed quite near to Pryor. But he was talking with another Mexican, and the Rio Kid waited until Mireles lay down, rolling up in a blanket for a nap. Pryor slouched over and stretched out a yard from Celestino.

"Celestino!" he whispered. "Make no move to draw attention!"

The lad's brown eyes opened wide. He started, but he kept his voice down.

"General! Why — What — How —"

"I came in with the stolen stock," Pryor told him. "Where kin we talk?"

"Follow me, but carefully," ordered Mireles.

He rose and sauntered over behind a group of hovels at the west side of Las Cuevas. The Rio Kid strolled after him, made the shelter of the shadows. He found Celestino awaiting him back of a big unlighted, windowless adobe brick building.

"We talk here," said Mireles. "Ees storehouse. No one weel hear, General! You hav' done dangerous theeng, comin' here. Ees death eef zey tak' you. Queeck, what ees wrong?"

"They've got Conchita Purcell a pris'ner here! Find where she is. I aim to take her out."

Swiftly Pryor sketched the events that had occurred since he had last seen his comrade.

"I too have foun' *mucho*," Mireles reported. "Ees someone een Texas who work weeth Gonzales an' Vance, *si*. Someone who sent word McNelly was here. All at Las Cuevas knew. Zey hav' grown bold. Zey mak' *mucho dinero* sellin' beef, *si*. Now zey hav' zis beeg herd, zey weel lie low teel McNelly go 'way."

"And the Black Heart murder business?"

"Zat's why I am steel here, General. I hav' not yet foun' all I weesh. Gonzales savvies. So do Vance. But no othairs here I hav' foun'. Ees somethin' to do weeth *el jefe,* ze chief, in Texas, I theenk. Why, General, why should zey want so great a range?"

"What yuh mean?" Pryor demanded, startled.

"I hav' foun' sev'ral peons, poor vaqueros here, who hav' sign' over certain claims to Gonzales an' Vance. Why?"

"Yeah? Where are these claims? What're they for?"

"I theenk ees for a great Spaneesh land grant, geeven two hund-red year ago."

"Huh, this was New Spain then. How far's this here grant go, d'yuh savvy?"

Celestino shrugged. "Of zat I am not sure, General. But far across ze Rio eento Texas."

"Would she take in Smithville, yuh figger?"

"*Si,* easily. And yet, zees lan' ees dry, ees covaire weeth chaparral, good only for graze' cattle. I weesh to know why Vance and Gonzales and *el jefe,* ze chief een Texas, go so far."

"We've got to find where Conchita is, first of all."

"Wait, I come back pronto," Pryor's companion said, low-voiced.

Celestino darted off. He was back within ten minutes.

"*Si,* she ees pris'ner in zat hut to ze south."

The Kid peered the way Mireles pointed. A small thatched hut, set near the palisades in the shadow, stood with door closed. A bravo slouched on guard outside.

"How many guards?"

"One outside. Ees senora weeth her een-side. But zere ees small gate right behind ze hut, General."

"Too many hombres around for us to git her out now," growled Pryor. "Here's how we'll do it, Celestino. I'll start trouble that'll draw ev'rybody away from that shack, savvy? Yuh kin take care of that bravo on guard. Slip in, fetch Conchita outa there and take her to the Rio, cross-country. Meet me in the brush south of the crossin'."

"*Si*, I do eet, life or death."

Mireles pressed his general's hand, swung away. He would get horses out, close up to the little gate behind that hut.

The Kid waited while Mireles hurriedly went outside. The lad was gone for only a short time. When he returned, he looked toward the spot where Pryor waited.

Then Celestino sauntered to the shack where the bravo sat on guard, and slid behind it. Now he was unfastening the little gate. Celestino reappeared. Taking off his sombrero, he wiped his face, signaling that he was ready.

Bob Pryor, chin down, walked toward the main gates. General Juan was still there. So was Gonzales, smoking a long brown cigarette and talking with lieutenants, tough bravo bosses of the bands raiding Texas.

The Kid slipped past to one side. They hardly glanced at the apparent peon. But his keen eyes photographed these *jefes* for future attention. He made his way into the shadows, and quickly found Saber, waiting for him.

Mounted on the swift dun, the Rio Kid knew he must make things loud and hot, or Mireles would never get Conchita out. He ripped off the Mexican sombrero, discarded the serape, put on his own hat.

Swiftly the juggernaut of Fate was rolling toward the terrific gamble of the Rio Kid. Guns checked and ready, he spurred the dun into the circle of firelight. He let out a war-whoop that startled the bravos.

"Who ees?" cried Gonzales, bounding forward, staring at the moving figure on the dun. "Ze Rio Keed!"

A grin on his lips, the Kid beat Gonzales to the draw. Both guns roared, but the Mexican's bullet zipped dirt yards in front of Saber. With a shriek of anguish, the bravo chief threw up his hands, collapsed in a heap with a slug through the brain.

146

Wails of fury rose, swelling to a great roar of hatred on the smoky air. Dancing with passion, the fighting bravos screamed for the blood of the Rio Kid.

But the Rio Kid's Colts were blasting them. His bullets ripped into two more, killing one, wounding the second. Men began rushing from the wide gates, milling in confusion, bumping against one another. Those in front threw up their pistols to kill Pryor.

Yet the slugs he sent shook their aim. He could not miss. Every bullet found a mark.

Moving all the time, the lithe Kid, warwhoop dominating the chorus of death, pivoted the dun. He flashed along the winding cattle trail that led southeast to Monterey, the main cattle depot where the stolen beeves were driven for sale to the army.

Bullets were screaming all around. Every bravo at Las Cuevas had only one thought — to kill the Rio Kid. Men and women came rushing out. Pursuit began almost instantly, Mexicans jumping on their hairy mustangs, taking Pryor's trail.

It was easy to pick off a man who, on a better mount, would get out too far in front of the mob. The night roared with the red-hot fury of the mob after the Kid, as he swiftly rode off.

The mad chase was strung out for a mile behind as more and more took to their saddles. But it picked up momentum. Tantalizing them with glimpses when he passed stretches bathed in moonlight, Pryor kept going.

For half an hour he kept up the game of tag. Then he knew that Mireles must have succeeded — or failed.

He urged the dun with his voice.

"Show 'em how a cayuse kin really run, Saber!"

Putting on a burst of speed, the Kid's pet showed them. He drew away rapidly, the yells and shots growing ever dimmer in Pryor's ears.

Gonzales and a couple of the bravo lieutenants were chalked up to his score in his campaign against the killers of the Rio. Pryor rode on for several miles before swinging north into the brush, headed for the Border.

Hours later, when the sun was well up, he saw the river through the mesquite. A mile south of Las Cuevas crossing, Mireles whistled to him from a patch of chaparral. The Mex had Conchita Purcell with him. The girl stood up, staring into the Kid's grim face. She suddenly burst into tears as he dismounted and took her hand.

"It was horrible," she sobbed.

He put an arm around her waist, comforting her.

"Who captured yuh?" growled the Kid, bleak fury in his heart at those who dared touch such a woman.

"I don't know. A blanket was thrown over my head. I wasn't far from the house, either, but someone crept up on me. After awhile I fainted, half smothered. I woke up in that shack at Las Cuevas."

Celestino nodded. "*Si*, General, all ees well. Tak' her back. You cross ze river now. Zere are American troops at ze ford. A young captain of cavalry follow ze rustlers to ze Rio."

"Yeah? I'll want a word with him. C'mon, Conchita. We'll find the Rangers, too — and Dan."

Celestino Mireles helped her on her horse, the one he had taken for her.

"Comin'?" the Rio Kid asked his friend.

Celestino shook his head.

"I go back to Las Cuevas."

"Huh? Why, they'll kill yuh."

"No, Senor," replied Mireles softly. "I am only a peon boy who ride out to chase you las' night. Now, I come back home."

"Didn't the guard see yuh?"

"*Si* — but he sees no more! As for ze senora who guard' Senorita Purcell, she was asleep. She wak', but ze hut was dark eenside. I am safe. I go back, find what I mus'."

They parted, the Kid taking Conchita with him, Mireles on his way back to Las Cuevas to gather information.

Over the great land brooded hate and death. Now the Rio Kid must fight alone against vast hordes of the enemy.

CHAPTER XIV
MCNELLY'S MEN

Under Captain L. H. McNelly's orders, Dan Worrell and the other Texas Rangers were cleaning their rifles and pistols. They were a good many miles east of Las Cuevas Crossing. Brownsville was a long ride down-river to the southeast. Fort Ringgold, with its barracks, lay ten miles upstream. North-east was Edinburg, with a third cavalry detachment of U.S. troops quartered there.

They had chased that bunch of hard riding gunmen for hours through the tortuous trails of the chaparral. Unimpeded by stolen stock and mounted better than the Rangers, the gunnies had stayed out ahead, tantalizing the Rangers with enough glimpses to force McNelly and his men to keep after them, but never stopping for a real clash. So little damage had been done to either side in the running battle that there seemed to be no sense to it.

At dark the pursuit had stopped, since

there was no way to trail the gang with any chance of taking them. The men who had fired on McNelly's command had swung south. They could cross the Rio Grande in the night or they might lurk in the thickets, ready to resume the fight in the morning.

But with the dawn the enemy had evaporated.

Worrell's strong face was grimly set. He was none too happy about his chances in life. Purcell had soured on him, and Conchita loved her father dearly. Worrell didn't want to come between the girl and her dad. Though he knew Conchita would run away with him any time, that she loved him and would sacrifice her life for him, he wouldn't ask her to do that. His ranch and belongings had been burned. All he owned were the clothes he had on, a few dollars, and his guns. Joining McNelly had been the one way he could get revenge on the men responsible for his plight. Also, he could earn a little money, forty dollars a month, while he tried to clean the thieves out of Texas so he could make a fresh start.

He kept thinking about Bob Pryor, the Rio Kid. The way Pryor brought him out of Belle Starr's had convinced him that the Rio Kid was one grand hombre. But what happened later had made him sad.

"I don't believe he'd kill anybody," Worrell muttered.

Sighing, he looked up.

Then he saw the spare, tall Captain Mc-Nelly coming toward the lounging Rangers. They would die for him and they knew he would never order them to go anywhere he wouldn't go first himself. That was Mc-Nelly. He treated them as he would his own sons.

There was a wrinkle between the captain's mild eyes. Even in the field, McNelly kept himself spick-and-span. Lieutenant Robinson was walking at his side, and Robinson signaled the men to gather around.

"Well boys," McNelly said in his soft way, as though about to deliver them a sermon, "I'm beginnin' to think I've been made a fool of. Here we are, miles down-river from Las Cuevas Crossing, and we didn't even get those attackin' bandits to stand and fight! Why was that attack made on us yesterday? I don't know. But I do know we can't fight these thieves the way they'd like us to. There're too many of 'em, and they know the land better'n anybody else. We gotta trap 'em like rats."

The Rangers listened intently. They were ready for anything the captain ordered.

"There are U.S. Army troops at Browns-ville, Edinburg and Ringgold barracks," went on McNelly. "We have thirty men, and that's not so many. The Mexicans can bring out hundreds of bravos in a scrap. However, I consider each one of you worth a whole passel of Mexes. It's the Army's business to keep this country pacified. The Mexican government can't do it. You all know that Porfirio Diaz has his hands full with revolts. He's trying to consolidate Mexico, and chaos is the result."

"What yuh aim to do, Cap'n?" a big Ranger asked. "Whatever it is, we're agree-able. We'll march to Mexico City if yuh give the word."

"Yes, I know you will," replied McNelly softly. "And — Well, all I'll say now is, we may do that, boys. Get your horses groomed and ready. Make sure your guns are in shape. We'll go back to the wagons and load up with food."

McNelly had brought provisions in mule-drawn wagons, which were left in camp when the Rangers rode to fight.

Quickly mounted, they started back up the Rio Grande. It was November but quite warm, the sun beating hot on their wide Stetsons.

Dan Worrell, mounted on a powerful stallion because of his weight, rode a short distance behind McNelly and Robinson. Young Bill Callicott chatted gaily at his side. Old Casuse was out in front, watching for spies to catch and bring back.

Half the distance back to Las Cuevas Crossing, the Rangers heard a hail from Casuse. Immediately they were on guard. McNelly spurred ahead, and Robinson signaled the men to come up. Worrell rode slightly behind Callicott. Dust whirled up from the beating hoofs.

Worrell recognized the rider Casuse had encountered. George Purcell's eyes were underlined, his face a mask of anguish. Sheriff Dave Carr and a couple of dozen men from Smithville rode with Purcell.

"Dan!" cried Purcell. "They've got Conchita, kidnaped her. Can't find her — They must've taken her across the river."

Dan Worrell nearly went insane. Fury clutched at him, and fear for his sweetheart.

"Damn them," he shouted. "I'll go over there! I'll go alone if I hafta —"

Captain McNelly pushed his horse over, put his slim hand on Dan's heaving shoulder.

"Keep your head, son," he ordered. "If we can, we'll get her back."

He snapped out commands, and the two

joined parties hurried west for the Crossing.

Worrell fought against the horrible fear in his heart. Conchita, a prisoner — perhaps dead. . . .

"I can't stand it," he muttered. But when he found McNelly watching him, he pulled himself together.

They had gone about three miles when the scouts ahead sang out. Riding near McNelly, Purcell and Carr at the head of the procession, Worrell stared in amazement. The Rio Kid and a second rider were coming swiftly toward them.

"Conchita!" Dan cried.

Spurring to her, he flung himself from his stallion to lift her down and press her to him.

Purcell's wide face broke into a relieved grin. He hurried to his daughter's side.

His clothing ripped and wet from the long ride and swim, Bob Pryor sat his saddle, one leg round the horn. A cigarette drooped from his lips. Sheriff Carr greeted Conchita. After asking her for information concerning her kidnaping, he swung on the Rio Kid.

"I don't know where yuh come into this, Pryor," the sheriff growled, "but yuh're wanted for that murder in Smithville."

"I'll go back some time and show yuh how

wrong yuh are," drawled the Kid. "Cap'n McNelly, I got some private information for yuh."

McNelly nodded, watching the sheriff and the Kid. Carr seemed unsure of what he should do. He glanced at McNelly. Pryor was alert, on guard. He had no intention of being taken a prisoner.

"S'pose," suggested the Ranger captain, "we let this charge hang fire till we're through with somethin' more important, Sheriff? It's my opinion yuh've made a mistake in the matter."

"Murder ain't no mistake. It's a crime," Carr replied coldly.

But he dared not try to take the Kid. Though he had his deputies along, McNelly was interceding for Pryor. Besides, Carr was aware of the fugitive's blinding speed in action.

Dan Worrell was ready to fight for his friend. He didn't care what came of it. Conchita had already told him how Pryor had snatched her from Las Cuevas. He started to push in, ready for a fight if Carr sought to arrest Pryor.

But McNelly brushed aside the sheriff's claim. "C'mon, Kid," he said. "I want the information you have for me."

Leading Pryor aside, he listened intently

to the Kid's report.

"That bunch of gunnies drawed yuh off, McNelly," the Rio Kid explained. "Then their pards crossed fifteen hundred head of stock to Las Cuevas. They're in their pens now, but they'll start for Monterey in a day or two. S'pose we cross and git 'em back? Gonzales is dead. Him and me had a little brush last night. I've spotted a bunch of the thieves' leaders, besides Sorreltop Vance, and I savvy the way to Las Cuevas."

"You're a brave man, Rio Kid," McNelly stated.

Pryor shrugged. "I scouted for Custer in the War, Cap'n — on a diff'rent side from you. But I got a lot of experience fightin' against yuh!"

The Ranger chief laughed.

"You believe we can finish 'em?" he asked eagerly.

"Yes. There's a hookup between the rustlers and them Black Heart murders, too. First thing is to smash the thieves. If we shoot down their leaders, that oughta impress 'em."

"You're right. I'm ready to cross the river."

"There's a young army cap'n at the ford now, McNelly. Randlett's his name. Company D, 8th Cavalry, is with him. He's planted a couple Gatling guns up on the

bank. Them thieves hit as far north as Edinburg, where he's stationed. Randlett tried
to catch up with 'em but they beat him to
the river."

"Mebbe we can use those troops," growled
McNelly.

"I wish yuh luck," Pryor said gravely.

"What d'you mean?"

Bob Pryor hesitated, for he realized what
a blow his information would be.

"Well, we rested awhile at Randlett's
camp, and a Major Clendenin, his superior
officer, comes tootin' along. The major says
the troops can't invade Mexico. It would
mean war. So Clendenin sends a note to
General Juan Flores, askin' for the cows
sent back with pink ribbons on their necks.
When I left they hadn't come yet."

McNelly snorted, but the Kid's dry wit
amused him too.

"I'll start over at dawn in a surprise attack, Rio Kid. Thanks for your boost and
great help."

"I'll go 'long," Pryor said, "if it's okay."

"Rather have you than another troop!
C'mon, ride with me to the Crossin'. It'll
keep you out of that dumb sheriff's way."

Giving orders to Lieutenant Robinson to
bring on the men, McNelly hastened west
for Las Cuevas ford. As they neared the

Crossing, McNelly turned to look at the Kid.

"What would you say, Pryor, if northern Mexico were added to the States?"

The Kid grinned. He knew how many Texans had thought of it. Sam Houston was one. Chaotic conditions in the southern land had put it into their heads. Only lately had the French pulled out of Mexico. Benito Juarez had won his long struggle against foreign oppression. But the moment the great leader died, a fight for power had begun at once, and young Porfirio Diaz was emerging on top.

Diaz had grown conservative. He was beating his enemies down, seizing all wealth and power in Mexico. Meantime the northern provinces were beyond his control. There was no stable government to right the wrongs against the Texans.

"An invasion," went on McNelly, "would bring on a war we could easily win. How about Cuevas, Kid? Are there any big shacks there, with thick walls, that a man could hold out in?"

"There's a storehouse. It's got loops for winders. A handful could hold it like the Alamo. I'm with yuh, McNelly."

"Once we're inside it," McNelly said, "American troops'll be forced to come over and rescue us."

They rode from the brush into the cavalry camp. Two Gatling guns faced the ford, sun gleaming on their burnished metal.

The Kid, a soldier still in heart, loved the camp. It reminded him of the exciting days of the War when he had been a squadron commander and scout. A bugle blew, and Saber snorted, for he had been trained in the army. Left in the picket line, he began bullying the army horses.

The Kid fraternized with the officers. But he listened with one ear while McNelly talked to Captain Randlett, a stalwart young officer. He heard Captain Randlett protesting vigorously.

"But my orders are not to cross the Border. The major forbade me. He's gone to the fort."

"Send a messenger for his permission." McNelly needed the troops to make the invasion official.

McNelly signaled the Kid, who ran up.

"Ride and fetch the boys, will you, Pryor?" Captain McNelly said, softly. "I'm goin' to try to get a hundred men from Randlett."

The Rio Kid mounted Saber, rode back and contacted Casuse. Then he returned to the Crossing.

"Any luck with Randlett?" the Kid asked.

McNelly shook his head. "No. Clendenin's stopped everything, Kid. Randlett's eager to fight, but says he'll come over only if he thinks our lives are in danger. The major wired General Potter, district commander at Brownsville, and the army's not to cross."

"Let's go ahead with the men we got," said Pryor.

"I'm goin' to," McNelly stated quietly.

CHAPTER XV
INVASION OF MEXICO

McNelly returned to the Ranger camp at midnight. Sheriff Carr and his posse had gone back to town with Conchita and Purcell, having accomplished their purpose of finding her. Dan Worrell stuck to his duty with the Rangers, despite his desire to accompany the girl.

The Rio Kid had been napping with the Rangers. He stood up, stretching, his lithe figure framed against the firelight.

He dropped his cigarette papers, stooped to pick them up. Just as he ducked his head, a rifle bullet smashed through his Stetson and plugged into the chaparral beyond. The sound of the gun was distant. Someone had been lying up on the hill, watching the Ranger camp. . . .

Swiftly the Rangers turned out. The Kid sent a shot back, but whoever sought to drygulch him had darted away into the night.

But there was no time for pursuit. Mc-Nelly was giving his orders before starting the march into Mexico.

"Boys, no surrender! We don't ask quarter or give it. We'll teach Mexico a Texas lesson."

The Kid and McNelly knew just what they were walking into. A handful of men was daring to pit itself against an army of Mexicans. Even if they could capture the storehouse at Las Cuevas, they would be killed unless troops came from the States to rescue them. In that way McNelly hoped to force a large-scale invasion.

The Rangers rode to the Crossing. On the bank above the cavalrymen were in bivouac.

"Here we go, boys," growled McNelly.

The Crossing was finally made after a long struggle. Then the Rio Kid began scouting the way toward the Mexican settlement. In the gray, threatening dawn, he saw the smaller ranch ahead, and knew that Las Cuevas was a half mile farther along.

On Saber he skirted out around the first ranch, so as not to alarm those inside. The attack on Cuevas demanded complete surprise to succeed. The Kid left the dun in a mesquite clump. Creeping toward the main gates of Las Cuevas, he heard the sound of gunshots behind him.

"They musta run into someone back there," he muttered, cursing the bad break.

In Las Cuevas, behind the big barred gates, people were already stirring. The corrals were filled with cows that must be driven to Monterey. Shooting from the other ranch increased in volume. The alarm broke at Las Cuevas.

Chagrined, the Kid heard their yells. Before long the gates burst open and fighting bravos emerged. He glimpsed Sorreltop Vance but held his fire. He wanted Vance alive if possible. He waited for McNelly to come up.

Hidden in the brush, he recognized a number of bravos who, he knew, were leaders of the raiding bands. They were the men to get.

He slid back nearer to Saber, standing silent in the chaparral. Shouts, gunfire, grew louder. McNelly at the head of his Rangers came charging up the dusty road from the Rio Grande. They had been discovered at the smaller ranch, Las Curchas, and had been forced to fight there, spoiling the surprise.

"Go for them, boys!" the Kid heard McNelly roar.

Rifle unshipped and ready, Pryor went into action. He rode along the flank of the

165

enemy facing the Rangers. His carbine snapped again and again as he picked off the leaders he had spotted. His accuracy from the moving dun was marvelous. One after another he sent slugs into the bravo chiefs.

Rattled by the stunning attack from an unexpected quarter, the growing army from Las Cuevas stopped their rush. They turned to fight back at the Kid. But McNelly and his men were charging, giving them no time to pause.

Fighting men went down. Screams of wounded rose with the banging volleys. Cool as ice, the Rangers used their needle guns to advantage, every shot hitting an opponent. The Mexes fell back toward their ranch, the Rangers after them. The Rio Kid was still taking his deadly toll.

A mad centaur raging against the foe, the great Rio Kid riddled them with his guns. He was like a wraith in the bush. His every shot meant death to the foe.

They were crowding back into the fortified village. The Kid, pressing them on, suddenly heard shouts from the Monterey road. Swinging in his sweated leather, he saw several squadrons of Mexican cavalry galloping toward Las Cuevas.

He had to report that to McNelly. With a

final smashing volley from his Colts, ignoring the dozen nicks and scratches from bullets he had received, he dashed back to the Rangers. The gates of Las Cuevas were being swung shut. McNelly's plan had failed.

"Mexican troops comin' up, Cap'n," the Kid reported. "About three hundred, I'd say. They're closin' the gates."

McNelly cursed in fury.

"It'd be suicide to attack now," he cried. "We'll have to retreat to the river."

The Kid stayed in the rear guard, fighting against bolder bravos who sought to pick off the retreating Rangers. When he got a few more of the lieutenants he was after, he had cleaned up a good percentage of them.

At the Rio Grande, he found McNelly was not figuring on crossing back to Texas.

"They'll figger we're scared and swimmin' the river, boys," McNelly growled. "Line up and we'll wait for 'em here."

The Kid swung the dun, rode through the brush near the trail. The beat of many hoofs came to him. He saw General Juan Flores Salinas coming in pursuit, at the head of fifty bravos. They were so sure the Rangers were in the water, easy prey, that they rode up in a bunch. Almost on the dropping bank, the Ranger captain roared:

"Fire!"

The Rio Kid took aim at Flores. Ranger guns blasted a murderous volley, and the Kid's Colt blared. General Juan Flores threw up his arms, clutching at his throat. He crashed from his horse, dying before he hit the dirt. When a dozen others had taken lead, the charge broke. A shriek of fury rose as they saw their *alcalde* die. Flustered, disheartened, they swung and started to retreat.

But, reinforcements up, they came again at the Rangers. The Kid shot from his point of vantage. He picked off three more bravos he wanted.

Six times they charged, and each time left dead and dying in the field. At last, terrified by the guns of the Rio Kid and the Rangers, they drew off. Yelling curses, but ever growing in numbers, they watched the men at the river.

The Kid was bleeding from his wounds, blackened by powder smoke and dust, when he trotted the proud dun back to the Rangers. McNelly seemed cool as the Kid himself. Plainly, he had no intention of surrendering.

"Yuh ain't goin' back, are yuh?" asked Pryor, dismounting.

"No," snapped McNelly. "C'mon, boys, dig in."

Across the Rio, Randlett watched the fight. He was surrounded by his troopers.

"For God's sake, Randlett, help us or we'll be wiped out!" McNelly bawled.

The Kid grinned. McNelly was acting to force the cavalry over. Firing suddenly burst again from the enemy, infuriated by the death of General Juan Flores and the bravos the Kid had slain. Bullets whistled over the Rangers, but the Mexicans did not attack again.

McNelly's mock distress was enough for Captain Randlett. He started his men over, coming at the head of the troop.

"Soon as your troopers are here," the Ranger cried, "we'll shove the Mexes right past Las Cuevas."

But Randlett shook his head stubbornly.

"I can't do that," he shouted. He wanted to fight but dared not disobey direct orders. "I'll stay with you till Major Alexander comes. General Potter sent him to take over command from Clendenin."

"We've got to have those cows, Cap'n," the Rio Kid yelled.

But Randlett would not advance farther into Mexico, though he knew that a first-class war was in the making as the troopers came over and lined up with the Rangers. Bullets whistled from both sides.

"Say, those are reg'lar Mexican troops back there," exclaimed Randlett. "I've got to return to Texas, McNelly. I'll be court-martialed for this."

But the Mexicans, hundreds on hundreds in battle array before them, did not charge.

"I've got to get back. Come on," urged Randlett.

"Look!" exclaimed the Rio Kid. "They're wavin' a flag of truce!"

"You take it, Randlett," growled McNelly, wishing this to be official.

The army captain accepted the message, written hastily by a Mexican *alcalde* who had taken General Flores' place.

"Says the cattle will be returned to Fort Ringgold tomorrow," shouted Randlett. "It asks us to withdraw our troops from Mexican soil."

"That means they're beaten," the Kid said. "Beaten and afraid. All we have to do is stay here to win."

"He's right," cried McNelly.

"Okay. We'll give 'em a truce till tomorrow."

McNelly nodded. "They must retreat three miles back from my picket line. I agree to give them one hour's notice before I attack!"

McNelly, the Rio Kid and Captain

Randlett, could now catch their breath. Food was brought over.

Late in the afternoon, Major Alexander arrived and hailed them from Texas soil. Complaints had been sent to Washington and Alexander had orders for Randlett to return at once.

Not daring to disobey any longer, Randlett started his troops back to American ground.

"It's all off," McNelly told his Rangers. "We can't get any men. Well, we'll stay here awhile."

"They can't surround us with the river at our back," observed Pryor.

Pickets out, the handful spent the night on the Mexican side.

By morning the wires were burning up between Mexico City and Washington. McNelly was advised to surrender or to return at once to Texas. No help was to be given him by the army.

"We'll stay here," McNelly decided.

"No wonder we had such a tough time winnin' the Civil War," jested Bob Pryor. "You was on the other side, McNelly!"

At four P. M. the Rio Kid was getting restless.

"Let's hit 'em," he suggested. "I b'lieve they'd run."

"Okay. I agreed to give 'em one hour, so

here goes."

The Rio Kid carried the message to the leaders of the Mexicans. Two thousand men were collected there, bravos, ranchers, several troops of regular cavalry. He could tell that they were rattled, fearful of McNelly's next move.

Coolly smoking a cigarette, the Kid parleyed under a white flag of truce with the new *alcalde*.

"Cap'n McNelly gives yuh one hour's notice," he drawled. "Then we attack, 'less yuh agree to our conditions, *alcalde*. First, we want them cows, with no red tape. We want 'em instantly started back to Texas. Second, we want Sorreltop Vance and what bravo chiefs of the rustlers yuh can catch. And third, a promise yuh won't harbor any more cattle thieves."

"I mus' talk weeth my *amigos,*" the *alcalde* retorted.

The Kid shrugged, blew out some smoke. Pivoting Saber, he rode slowly back to McNelly.

"They'll quit," he told the Ranger.

A few minutes later commissioners arrived from the Mexican forces. They agreed to McNelly's conditions.

Having won against impossible odds, McNelly started his forces back to Texas. They went into camp a short distance east of the Crossing.

"If they don't bring those steers over by tomorrow," McNelly declared, "I'll go after 'em."

"I'll go with yuh," the Kid grinned. "I reckon we smashed them cow thieves for the time bein', McNelly. The Mexes'll be so scared now that they'll chase into the chaparral anybody they don't hand over to us."

Tired and victorious, the Rangers cooked up a hot meal. Night fell over the vast Rio Grande country.

After supper, a dark figure that had slipped up to the Ranger pickets was fetched to the firelight. The Kid leaped to his feet. It was his friend, Celestino Mireles, clothes dripping.

"Celestino," cried Pryor, pumping his pal's hand. "What's up?"

McNelly came over to listen.

"Go ahead," ordered the Kid. "This is Cap'n McNelly, Celestino. He's the head of the Rangers."

"*Bueno,*" exclaimed Mireles. "We hav' won, General, *si.* I come from Las Cuevas. Zey are smash'. Zey drive out ze rustlers. Zey try to arres' zem, but Sorreltop Vance line two hunderd up. Zey go 'way weeth zeir

173

guns, bravos and outlaws from Texas. Mos' of ze lieutenants are dead. I hear Vance say he weel meet — hees chief *een Texas!*"

Chapter XVI
Big Foot

Growling with pleasure, McNelly had listened intently to the Mexican spy's report.

"Any idea where Vance and his cattle thieves mean to meet this chief of theirs?" the Ranger captain asked.

"*Si.* I hav' work' hard, senors. Ees near Smeethville, not far from zis spot. Vance has sent word to Senor Juan Hardin to come help zem."

"Hardin!" exclaimed McNelly. "Why, I'd ride every horse to death to capture John Wesley Hardin! He's the kind I don't want in Texas!"

"What d'yuh say, McNelly?" the Rio Kid drawled. "I'll go ahead to Smithville and look over the lay of the land. S'pose yuh pretend yuh're leavin' and march west. Then connect with me this side of town, in the chaparral Camp jest south of the trail and watch for me."

"It's a deal," McNelly agreed. "Tomorrow

I mean to get the stolen cows back. After that I'll be happy to smash Vance and those cattle thieves. But right now we'd better turn in."

At the crack of dawn, the Rio Kid was spruced up. He felt himself again. He rode northeast from the Ranger camp with Celestino Mireles and Dan Worrell. Now that the worst of the fighting was over, Worrell was anxious to return to Smithville and find out how his sweetheart was.

The Rio Kid and Captain L. H. McNelly had crushed the cattle thieves in Mexico. Sobered by the death of General Flores, appalled at the incredible nerve of McNelly and his men, the Mexican villagers would no longer give sanctuary to the cattle thieves. They had driven them out, fearing a return of the Kid and McNelly. The wholesale beef market would no longer get its supplies from Texans via the Mexes.

The three young men made a quick run for Smithville. Mireles spoke with the Rio Kid as they rode.

"General, I learn' much while at Las Cuevas. Gonzales an' Vance force many peons zere to sign papers for zero. I tol' you zere ees great Spaneesh grant here. Eet tak' een hundreds of square miles, one, two counties. Smeethville ees part of eet."

"I know 'bout those grants," said the Kid. "There were sev'ral of 'em. But they don't all hold good, Celestino. Texas has changed hands."

"Ees right, but many do, General. All zis countree once belong' to ze Jesuit fathers. Een seventeen-seexty-seven, ze Jesuits were arres' an' deport'."

The Kid nodded. He knew of the wholesale deportation of the Jesuits in the eighteenth century, after they had converted the wild Indian tribes and set them to work. The great land grants were then transferred to Spanish nobles. American law would still uphold some of these titles, provided there were not too many conflicting claims.

"You could never take over a whole town like Smithville," the Kid mused. "Not unless —" He broke off, slapped his leg, and spurred up to Dan Worrell.

The young giant's face was sad yet eager. He hoped that perhaps the antagonism against him might have abated somewhat. But he was even more anxious to see his sweetheart. Dan quickly answered the Kid's queries.

"Shore! Come to think of it, the folks who were kilt were all land owners, every one of 'em! Yeah, Purcell owns about a quarter of the town. He'd be dead hisself, on'y he's

177

managed to fight 'em off so far. Yuh know, he's keepin' a bunch of guards around the store."

They reached the hills overlooking the valley in which Smithville was set. That evening, the Rio Kid and Mireles hid themselves in their camp. Dan Worrell rode down to Purcell's, while it was still not dark.

The Rio Kid had purposely come to this point. He could see the section of the creek where he had made his escape. Wounded by the infuriated townsmen, he had crept into the underground canal.

"I wanta have a look-see down below, Celestino," he drawled. "I been thinkin' all this over. I got a hunch why this here chief and Vance're so anxious to git their hands on that Spanish grant. If there ain't any conflictin' claims, they could take it all easy enough."

Mireles agreed to keep an eye on the trails for him. With a Winchester carbine across his knees, the Mexican lad took his stand up above the creek bed. He watched while Pryor descended through the chaparral and waded across the creek to the hidden canal entrance.

Pryor carried matches in a waterproof case and a couple of candles he had obtained from the Rangers. The Kid ducked into the

178

underground ditch and made his slow way along it. Coming to the spot where he had stopped to recuperate, he stuck his candle on a rock and began widening the opening where the wall had caved in. This took him only a few minutes, for the stones were loose and easily moved. He discovered old adobe cement that had dried on various bricks.

Shading his tiny flame from the draught, he proceeded. The ditch ran a long way, and he found it very tiresome crawling on hands and knees. But he went on for hundreds of yards. The canal had been cunningly pitched so that water from the creek could flow through it.

At last he came out into a round pool some yards in extent, and his light illuminated a higher ceiling of reddish rock. He could leave the water here, and stand erect.

"I was right," he muttered. "It's an old mine!"

The workings were remarkably large. As he wound through the passages, he saw the shrewdly engineered ditches that brought water for the use of miners. Indian miners, he knew, slaves who worked away their lives for the glory and enrichment of the Jesuits.

Crude tools, copper pans, covered with

the verdigris of a hundred years, lay where they had been hurriedly dropped. The notice of expulsion had come as a swift, terrible blow to the Jesuits. They warned the Indians never to reveal the gold mines they had found, on pain of excommunication and death. Superstitious fear kept the Indians from pointing out the old mines. And by then they had realized that gold meant they would be enslaved by the whites. Now, after so long, few natives knew where the ancient gold mines lay.

All this the Rio Kid knew, as he knew the strange history of his native land, Texas, once part of old Mexico.

He heard vague murmurings, but could not place them for a time. The ground seemed shaky overhead, and he looked up. Bits of clay or a pebble would now and again drop from the roof.

"By golly," he muttered. "Smithville's right over me! That's folks I hear, in their houses! Town's built over part of the mine."

A moment later, around a sharp turn in a gallery, he saw the yellow flame of a lantern. As he sought to jump back and douse his candle, he recognized the evil face of Sorreltop Vance.

"Hey — who's that? Halt or I'll fire!"

Several others were with Vance. The Kid

glimpsed dark-faced bravos, cattle thieves from Mexico, bunching behind the redhead.

There must have been other entrances to the mine. But he had no time to figure this out. He heard Vance shout:

"Chief, there's a spy in here! Quick, let's take him, boys!"

The pursuit rushed forward. In the confined space under the earth, pistols boomed with deafening power. Pryor fired back once, to slow them up. He dashed full-tilt for the pool, to make his escape.

He reached the pool well ahead of them, plunged in. He pushed on hands and knees into the rock-lined tunnel that led to the creek. For a short time he could hear them calling to each other, splashing around, hunting him. Then he reached the outside.

It was dark when he scrambled across the creek and went up the hill. Mireles was awaiting him there.

"Now I got the answer," Pryor told his Mexican friend.

The Rio Kid knew that a big battle was impending. One man's cunning brain attempted to gain full control of the vast Spanish grant and the gold mine of the Jesuits under it. Now that sinister foe was swiftly gathering his forces for a wholesale killing.

"I reckon," Pryor told Celestino, in the warming sun of the following morning, "that he'll make one big stab so's to clean up these heirs. Purcell's evidently one, and that means Conchita, too, her bein' his daughter."

"And ze Black Heart? Why ees zat?"

Pryor shrugged. "You savvy yore own folks, Celestino. Anything like that'll scare 'em silly, worry 'em so they'll quit. Plenty of people have left Smithville already, and more'll go with ev'ry Black Heart killin'. Not only is it cover for the murderer, but it helps him clear the grant of claimants."

"You are right, General," Celestino Mireles agreed. "But hear — Someone comes!"

They lay flat, silent, watching the trail. Their horses were back in the chaparral. Celestino's hairy mustang had been muzzled with a piece of sash so he would not whinny when he scented other horses.

Up the slope from Smithville, winding through the brush, came a man on a huge black horse. It took a large animal to carry the man's weight, for he was an incredibly powerful giant who must have weighed close to three hundred pounds. A beaver hat was cocked on his head, which was growing bald with age, and his blue eyes blinked unhappily. In fact, his whole demeanor seemed that of a manic depressive who has just had the most awful news.

"Big Foot Wallace?" breathed Pryor.

He knew the gigantic frontiersman well. Big Foot had assisted the Rio Kid in crushing a gang of killers who had taken over the local country after the Civil War.

The stir the Kid made as he got up warned Big Foot. He was instantly on guard, his Sharps rifle leaping to his hands. He had on fringed buckskin and moccasins.

"Who's in them bushes," he snarled, leveling the Sharps. "C'mon out and lemme see yuh, or I'll blow yuh to kingdom come!"

"Howdy, Big Foot," the Rio Kid sang out. "Better step in and have a bite with us."

"Well, by the great hornspoon," exclaimed Big Foot, as he saw the Kid's smiling face peering at him from the chaparral. "If it ain't the Rio Kid! How are yuh?"

Big Foot slid off the big black, and pulled his animal into the bush after him, dropping reins to ground to pump the Kid's hand in a warm greeting.

He knew Mireles, too, and greeted him.

"Let's go back here where we kin talk, Big Foot," Pryor suggested. "We're sorta on the dodge in these parts and don't wanta be seen."

"What's up?" asked Wallace, as he trailed

them to their camp.

The Kid quickly told him.

"I'll be hornswoggled if I don't stick around and help yuh," Big Foot declared. "I'm that mad I could kill a whole passel of outlaws, Kid!"

Big Foot squatted down, chewing on refreshments Pryor passed out generously.

"What's wrong?" inquired the Rio Kid. "I noticed yuh looked sorta unhappy, Big Foot."

"I got a right to be. Yuh know that big Lipan Indian I been after for so many years?"

"Yeah."

Bob Pryor had heard the tale of Big Foot's nickname. Many years ago Wallace had started slaying raiding Indians. One night he ran onto the marks of tremendous moccasins, sixteen inches in length. Big Foot had made it his ambition to hang these huge footgear on his cabin wall, with other trophies such as Apache and Mexican scalps. He had spent most of his spare time chasing the Lipan.

Alas, after raiding all around Texas, the Lipan had dropped out of sight. Everybody knew about Wallace's obsession to possess those vast moccasins, and the frontiersmen all sympathized with him.

"Lemme tell yuh," Big Foot continued dolefully, "what happened, Kid. I been drivin' the mail from El Paso to San Antonio through six hunderd mile' of Apache wilderness. I shore had some fine sport fightin' savages, I'll tell yuh. But that's nuthin'.

"One trip I'm headed east and almost to San An, and I stop to water my mules. Right there in the sand I see that big Lipan's track! I near went loco, Kid. I hadn't seen it for ten year', but I knowed it. So I turned off and drove to a friend of mine, Jerry Westfall, an old-timer like me. I give him warnin' that this Lipan thief was around. 'Sure as hell's hot,' I says to Westfall, 'that Lipan'll git all yore stock. Now if yuh git him, I want his moccasins,' I says, and Jerry agrees."

Big Foot paused, and took a swig of whiskey from his flask.

"Well?" grinned the Kid.

"I hadda deliver my U.S. mail, no matter what. And Westfall says if he gits the Lipan, I git the moccasins, him savvyin' how I felt all these years. Shore enough, the Lipan runs off all the stock around and I had to lend 'em mules to chase him. Westfall trails him for a week and suddenly Jerry sees the bush move up ahead. He throw up his Sharps and — *bang!*"

"Was it the Lipan?" asked the Kid interestedly.

"Shore!" the giant snarled unhappily.

"Well, didn't yuh git the moccasins Westfall promised yuh?"

Big Foot shook his head dolefully. There were actually tears forming in his eyes.

"Westfall kept his word, Kid. He sent them moccasins to me at San An, but I'd jest pulled out with the mail for El Paso. Some dirty skunk from the east, huntin' souvenirs, swiped 'em from the office. That's after I been huntin' that thief for ten years! I'm in a savage mood, Rio Kid. I'll be hornswoggled if I wouldn't exterminate a whole army if there was even only a pretty fair reason."

"Stick with us," promised the Kid, "and yuh'll have yore chance, Big Foot! We're tacklin' the biggest army of sidewinders —"

"I hear somebuddy comin' from the west!" Wallace announced, pricking up his keen frontiersman's ears. "And they're moving plenty cautious —"

CHAPTER XVII
THE KID
SCOUTS AGAIN

On the alert instantly, the three men started to creep toward the trail. Lying flat in the mesquite on the ridge, they watched a band of fighting men approach. Pryor had hoped it might be McNelly and his Rangers, coming to keep the appointment the captain had made with the Rio Kid.

Instead they saw a couple of dozen rough looking Texans. Pryor immediately recognized them. He had seen them at Belle Starr's lonely shack in Hell's Gate, which had been a depot for the cattle thieves until the Kid's warning caused Belle to depart.

In the midst rode John Wesley Hardin, the desperado. His thin face was set in a mask of cold ferocity, his clothes dirty and ragged.

"S'pose we pull out here and wait till Vance connects with us, Hardin?" a gunny suggested, as they came near to the hiding place of the Kid and Big Foot. "We don't wanta show our faces in Smithville 'fore the attack."

"Right," Hardin snapped. "I have a bone to pick with that skunk they call the Rio Kid. Vance says he's still around and this time I'll beat him to the draw. I shore wish Belle had stayed to see it."

"Well, she didn't," growled the other. "She lit out for Indian Territory, and I can't say I blame her none. With the Kid and McNelly in the country, I don't feel none too safe myself. The Mex market is busted high, wide and handsome, thanks to them. I'd hate to have McNelly on my trail, and that Rio Kid ain't no slouch hisself."

"I'll kill him," promised Hardin, "when I see him again."

They were starting to dismount, evidently intending to lie up in the brush until they heard from Sorreltop Vance. The Kid figured they must have had a message from Vance, asking them to help him in crushing Smithville. The chief was marshaling his forces of evil, for the greatest battle of all was approaching.

From behind them, the trio heard the sudden whicker of a horse. They had neglected to muzzle Wallace's black. The sound instantly warned the party with John Wesley Hardin.

"What the hell —" the leader gasped.

"Let's go git 'em," whispered Big Foot Wallace in the Rio Kid's ear.

A rear guard came spurring up full-tilt.

"Hey, boys, I seen the Rangers! They're headin' this way. McNelly's with 'em."

"McNelly! He's bad medicine — Quick, let's hide in the brush!"

The gunnies started straight toward the hidden three. Hardin was protected by the bodies of his mates. The three jumped up, giving the Rebel yell, and Big Foot could beat any Indian at a war-whoop.

Three guns flashed, booming in the hills. Three of the outlaws left leather, dead before they landed.

"It's the Rio Kid!" a man shrieked.

They fell back before the guns of Big Foot, Celestino and the Rio Kid. Panic seized the men in the trail. They turned and fought for a chance to escape. McNelly was coming up. They feared not only the Kid but the Ranger captain. Hardin was aware that the Rangers were on his trail. He glimpsed the set face of Bob Pryor, who sought to settle things with the badman.

Hardin sent a swift shot that nipped a chunk of leather from the Kid's chap leg. Pryor fired, and Hardin's hat, the only part of the desperado visible to Pryor, jumped.

189

The badman rode right out from under it.

Leaping out in a last attempt to get a clear bead on his foe, the Kid glimpsed the drawn, pale face of John Wesley Hardin. Low over his horse's mane, the bandit hit for the tall timber. Pryor's parting shot was stopped by a horseman who spurred between the Rio Kid's deadly pistol and the fleeing Hardin.

With a curse of disappointment, Bob Pryor saw John Wesley Hardin make the turn and drop out of his range of vision. The trail was a mess of running mustangs, bumping against one another in an effort to escape.

It was to be the Rio Kid's last glimpse of Hardin, although he did not know it then. He never again came face to face with this notorious badman, said to be the worst of them all, a killer who would shoot a man just to see him kick. The Texas Rangers, Mc-Nelly's declaration that he would run Hardin to the finish, the fury of the Rio Kid, sent John Wesley out of Texas.

For three years Hardin hid himself under an alias in Florida. But Lieutenant J. B. Armstrong, one of McNelly's able successors, brought him back to Texas where he was sentenced to life imprisonment at hard labor. Hardin refused to perform manual labor. Punishment had not feazed him when, in 1893, he was pardoned and released. He seemed to be going straight for a time, but he returned to his old ways of life. He was shot dead by John Selman two years later.

Blue smoke puffs wafted up on the warm Texas air. Explosions banged in the hills. Then the screams of a wounded horse drowned out every other sound.

"Fetch the horses, Celestino," bawled the Rio Kid, shooting as fast as he could from the trail.

The desperados swung northwest, away from Bob Pryor and the line of march of Captain L. H. McNelly. The Rangers, about two miles distant, came slowly to meet the Rio Kid at the designated rendezvous.

Up on the ridges above Smithville and its creek valley, the thick chaparral made pursuit difficult. Though Big Foot Wallace, the Rio Kid, and Celestino Mireles performed miracles of riding and shooting, there were but three of them. So they were able to account for only a few of the gang which had been coming down with Hardin to join Sorreltop Vance and his chief in their attempt to crush Smithville.

Torn by thorns, covered with dust and sweat, bleeding from flesh wounds, the trio in the rear finally gave up the chase. They started south to intercept Captain McNelly.

Old Casuse and the captain were riding out in front as the Rio Kid hailed them. Big Foot Wallace pulled up his black horse, throwing one great leg around his saddle-horn to ease his seat.

The Mexican Ranger grinned at the Kid.

"What for you shoot, hey, Rio Keed? You killum?"

"*Si, si,*" the Kid replied, flashing his teeth. "Yuh missed the fun, Casuse." He turned to McNelly. "Did the cattle come back to Texas?"

"Yes, but we had to cross over to Mexico to hustle 'em up, Pryor. We didn't bag many thieves, though. They rode out with Sorrel-top Vance, as your friend reported. Have you been able to locate Vance for me? If we can smash him and his gang, it'll finish the rustlers for good."

"Shore have, Cap'n," the Rio Kid replied. "He's hidin' on the other side of Smith-ville."

"Then let's hit him and get it over with."

"Cap'n McNelly," Pryor said earnestly, "if they find yuh're here, they'll jest scatter and leave for the high timber. Will yuh give me a chance to trap 'em? I reckon I kin do it if I have a little time."

McNelly shrugged. He was pale under his coating of tan. The Ranger chief, the greatest of them all, was holding himself up by sheer willpower. He had but a few short years to live.

"Okay, Rio Kid. A rest won't do us any harm. What's your idea about this job?"

"S'posin' yuh go into camp in the brush, keep pickets out and make shore yuh ain't seen? I'll scout 'round the town tonight and locate the enemy. Mebbe we kin surround 'em. Or if they're on the prowl, why, I'll prod 'em up and lead 'em into yore arms."

McNelly approved. The long strain of the Las Cuevas battle had been terrifically wearing on all concerned. He shook hands with Big Foot Wallace, an old-timer with whom he was acquainted.

"Glad to see you, Big Foot," he said. "I wish you'd been along on the Las Cuevas party."

"Me, too," Big Foot agreed.

Wallace was one of the survivors of the ill-fated Mier expedition. Two hundred Texans, in reprisal for a raid by Mexican soldiers during the Texas War for Independence, had marched to Mier, Mexico, and tried to capture the country. Running short of ammunition, the Texans had been made prisoners. They had escaped, only to be recaptured.

One hundred and seventy-five had been lined up in the plaza of the Mexican town, and forced to draw beans from a sombrero. One bean in ten was black, and whoever drew a black one was summarily shot as punishment for the escape. Big Foot's luck had held. He had got a white one, and lived to kill more than his share of Indians, his present specialty.

"What was all the shootin' we heard as we came up?" inquired McNelly.

Pryor explained. At mention of John Wesley Hardin, McNelly could not tolerate delay.

"C'mon, let's get him!" he said.

"No use, Cap'n. He had a strong, fresh horse and his trail's covered by a bunch of others. He's miles away by now. He ain't comin' back where we kin take him. Yore horses look mighty jaded to me."

"That's true. They are done in." McNelly bit his lip in disappointment. "Next time," he muttered. "I sent a message to Captain Richard King, owner of the big Santa Gertrudis Ranch. A lot of those stolen steers belong to him and I told him to send some cowboys over and drive the animals home. How many fightin' men do you s'pose this

Sorreltop Vance and his pals can muster?"

"Oh, two hundred or so, I reckon," answered Pryor.

"I'll be hornswoggled, Kid," exclaimed Big Foot Wallace delightedly. "If yuh don't take a man on the swellest parties! Last time we fit the Apaches and that gang belongin' to the Eagle. This trip I kin kill these Mex cow-thieves wholesale."

McNelly had some two dozen Rangers with him. The rest of his party was still at Rio Grande City, overseeing the return of the stolen cows to their rightful owners. There was not, in any of the men's minds, the least doubt that they could handle the two hundred bravos and renegades of Sorreltop Vance. It was only a question of getting close enough to clash with the foe.

"That gunfire must've been heard in Smithville," the Rio Kid declared. "Vance and his chief're sure to send out men to see what it was all about. So we better git under cover, Cap'n McNelly."

He led the way along a cattle trail that twisted narrow and tortuous through chaparral, across the mesquite ridge and down the slope toward the valley of Smithville. In the distance they could just glimpse the roofs of the town. The main trail from the west lay north of their position, cunningly chosen by the expert Pryor.

The Rangers had made a forced march from Rio Grande City. Their horses were lathered, coated with gray dust. The men unsaddled, rubbed down their horses, picketed them in grass, and went into camp. McNelly threw himself down on a blanket and closed his tired eyes.

But the Rio Kid could not rest. He rode Saber to the spot where the battle with Hardin had taken place. He quickly dragged a couple of dead stock thieves back into the brush, leaving them for the Mexican vultures and coyotes. Then he erased all signs of the fight.

Hardly had he finished when his keen ears caught the sharp sounds of horse hoofs clinking on the stony trail up from Smithville. He ducked back into the chaparral. Presently into his range of vision came a pair of hard-eyed riders. One was a Mexican bravo in steeple sombrero and fancy clothes. The other was a renegade Texan, some outlaw who had joined Sorreltop Vance's evil banners.

"Don't seem sensible to go pokin' 'round much further," the Texan growled to the Mex. "Mebbe them shots was some brush-popper killin' coyotes, Telesforo."

"*Si, si.* We go back, Beel, tell Senor Vance."

They rode only a little farther, then turned their mustangs and trotted back toward Smithville. Up on the ridge, climbing a stunted oak tree, the Rio Kid watched the trail their dust made. Now and then, from his eyrie, he could glimpse them as they threaded a way around the town. They dared not show themselves yet to the citizens. The Kid saw them make the chaparral to the northeast of Smithville, and then they dropped out of his vision.

"They'd've started within five minutes or so of the shootin'," he figured.

In that way he was able to approximate the distance Vance's hiding place must be from the town. He returned to the Ranger camp and lay down for a cat-nap, awaiting the cloak of night.

Big Foot Wallace was delighted when the Rio Kid asked him to go along on the scout.

"Shore enough, Kid," the giant frontiersman cried. "Drivin' the mail gits sorta monot'nous, even with the Apaches skunkin' the bush. I ain't been on a real expi-dishun for years. Let's git goin'."

They were smoking, after having eaten broiled beef and hardtack from the Ranger stores. That appetizing food had been washed down with strong coffee brewed in tin cans over the little, guarded fire they had built.

Celestino was rested after his escape from Las Cuevas with vital information for his friend, the Rio Kid. He, too, was to go along.

The trio started under the stars. The moon was only a glow on the horizon. They threaded through the brush and reached a trail which would take them to another that wound to the north of Smithville, whose lights were visible in the valley. Not far from those lights were the killers — and right toward them the small party of three rode!

Chapter XVIII
The Gunnies
Attack

Edging forward cautiously, the Kid rode in the lead, Mireles next, then Big Foot as rear guard. Like wraiths they shoved their rested horses into the creek valley. Taking the turn-off to the left, Pryor felt the branches of the bushes reaching for his leather, brushing the sides of Saber.

Up north of Smithville, the trail swung and crossed the creek. Their horses slid on the stony bottom. Then they clambered up the clay bank and rode again in the stunted jungle.

For another mile the Rio Kid kept on, at a northeast angle from Smithville. They could always place the town by the faint sky-glow of its many lamps.

He knew he was coming close to the hidden enemy camp. This he could estimate by his timing of Sorreltop's scouts that afternoon. Silently he gave the signal to stop, and the three came together. The Kid whispered to Mireles.

"Hold the horses, Celestino. Stick here where we kin pick yuh up, savvy?"

"*Si*, General," the Mexican youth replied. He wanted to be in the scrap. Though his dark eyes were disappointed, he would obey his friend.

"C'mon, Big Foot," ordered Pryor. "Leave yore rifle, but don't forgit yore knife."

"Why, I wear it insteada pajamas," grinned Wallace.

In buckskin and moccasins, the giant frontiersman could move without a sound through any sort of country. Trained to this sort of warfare, his favorite recreation was sneaking up on Apaches and Comanches.

Bob Pryor took off his spurs, changed his riding boots for deerskin moccasins he carried in his pack for the purpose. He left his Stetson hanging by its strap from Saber's saddlehorn. He quickly bound his chestnut hair with a strip of deerhide. In such work nothing must impede the scout. He had his gun stuck in his belt, his knife in front and all ready for use.

The Rio Kid slipped into the lead. Mireles, holding the reins of the three horses, sought to keep them quiet. He drew them into the brush, off the trail, and waited for his friends' signal.

The trail was black as ink where moved the Rio Kid and Big Foot Wallace. The soft sounds of their progress might have been the wind stirring the dry grass. With his hands, with scent and vision, with the strange sixth sense of a scout, the Rio Kid began hunting for the enemy.

They proceeded for a quarter of a mile without encountering the slightest hint of the foe's presence. Cunningly, Sorreltop Vance had hidden his hombres in the thick bush, until the moment would come to strike.

The Kid felt Big Foot touch his ankle. He paused, turning, and the giant breathed in his ear.

"There'll shore be a man watchin' this trail, Kid."

Pryor nodded. He had been looking for the sentry. Yard by yard they went on, stopping to listen, to sniff the cooling air.

Then the Rio Kid, slightly farther along, stopped. So certain was he of Big Foot's ability, that the Kid didn't bother to tell his friend that he had caught a whiff of cigarette smoke.

Flat on the earth the town men lay. Patiently they waited for the guard, hidden near the next turn, to indicate his exact position. They already knew, by the error the man had made in smoking on duty, that he was near at hand.

There were always cracklings of some sort in the dry chaparral. But the Rio Kid's trained ear could identify each sound. Small animals, insects, birds, moved in the darkness, yet he was able to single out one particular noise. At last he caught the shifting of the sentinel's feet. The creak of leather boots was another error on the part of the guard.

Inching on a bit at a time, Pryor drew in. He was rewarded by the faint red glow of an inhaled cigarette. It placed the sentry perfectly.

Now he put back his hand, touched Big Foot Wallace's. The scout was right with him. Big Foot understood the principles of this game. He waited there while the Rio Kid snaked past where the guard sat in the brush.

Carefully turning, Pryor deliberately made a slight noise, just enough to interest the sentry. It might have been a rabbit or a snake. But when it came again, the guard got up, looking along the trail in the Kid's direction. He saw the darker shadow the Rio Kid's body made against the earth. Before he could utter a sound, Big Foot struck.

Like a flying panther, the giant unerringly got the throat. They rolled onto the trail, and suddenly there was a sharp snap. The bravo's neck was broken. He lay weirdly quiet.

The Rio Kid jumped to the spot, felt the chaparral. Sticks in full leaf had been cut and then replaced in the sandy dirt, to conceal the entrance to the newly broken blind trail.

Hiding the guard's body in the chaparral, they started along the hidden path, careful to replace the brush screen.

Two hundred yards beyond, they came upon a sharp dip. Secreted in the hollow was the camp of Sorreltop Vance. A single fire, blanketed by a stone fireplace built against an overhanging shelf of red rock, sufficed for cooking. By its faint red glow the Kid and Big Foot, flat on their bellies, could look over the enemy encampment. Sleeping forms, wrapped in serape or blanket, were everywhere. A half dozen sentries lounged on rocks around the circle. Certain warning would come from the trail if any attack began.

"There's Sorreltop," breathed Pryor.

The red-headed devil he had been hunting so long was awake. Pryor hoped to take him a prisoner, and thus solve the enigma of the Black Heart murders. They saw him stretch his long arms, yawning as though just roused. Over in the shadows on the opposite side of the camp hidden from spying eyes, was a dark figure in a black cloak and a sombrero. Its face was muffled by the folds of the serape.

"The chief!" muttered the Rio Kid. It was the hombre he had seen near the Border.

Vance strolled over to him, squatted down at his side. The hum of their voices came to the listening Kid and Big Foot.

The chief seemed to be giving commands. Vance straightened up, and snapped orders to his guards. They began walking along the lines of sleeping fighters, roused them with well placed kicks in the ribs.

Figures sprang up, grabbing rifles and gun-belts. Sorreltop Vance stood in the center, motioning them around him.

"Time we got started," the redhead told them. "We're goin' to hit and hit hard, boys."

The two out in the bush could see the fierce, bearded face, catch the glint of the killer leader's terrible eyes.

"Make shore yuh got plenty of ammunition. I'll want fifty of yuh behind me first off to hit the store. Purcell's got six fightin' men in there, but we'll rush the place easy enough, and take it, too. The chief'll see that the front door's left unlocked, savvy? We'll be inside 'fore they know it. The rest of yuh scatter and don't spare yore guns. Remember, it's no quarter. If yuh wanta, and got time, set fire to the shacks. When the job's done, we'll all meet back here. Make shore yuh kill Dan Worrell right off."

The horrible plan to devastate Smithville, to wipe out the inhabitants in a wholesale massacre, was the final lash of the hidden chief. The Rio Kid had discovered that he was primarily after the great Spanish mine which ran under part of the town. If the title to the old grant could be cleared, the owner would be fabulously wealthy, an emperor of Texas. But to win, there must be no dispute about ownership of the vast tract. Litigation was expensive and likely to be drawn out for years, and the courts were inclined to favor the new holders of the land since the War for Independence.

The bravos were well armed with Winchester or Remington carbines. Besides, the Mexicans toted long knives, their favorite weapon for close fighting. Pockets began to bulge with cartridges as they scooped them up from the boxes opened in the center of the camp. Perhaps fifty of Vance's followers were renegade Americans. The rest were

Mexican bravos, killers and cattle thieves, deserters from Porfirio Diaz' army.

Two hundred desperadoes, about to descend upon the luckless people of Smithville, crowded the camp. The picket lines of mustangs were back to the north, in the chaparral, where there was evidently another way in to the hollow.

Blocked by the great array of fighting men, the Rio Kid hunted for the elusive hombre in the serape. But the chief was no longer in sight. He had slipped off into the velvet blackness.

Already the murderers were starting for the horses, to saddle up. Under Sorreltop's hand, they would then strike the Texas town.

There was no time to lose, the Kid realized. Such a foray would take but a short time. The citizens of Smithville were already sadly shattered by the Black Heart murders. They could not hold out in their scattered houses against the planned mass attack.

The Kid turned. The sounds Big Foot and he made were lost in the bustle of gunnies preparing for the fray. The two melted back along the narrow trail, ran at full-tilt for the place where they had left Celestino Mireles and their horses.

"Hustle, Celestino!" gasped Pryor, as the Mexican youth pulled the three mounts to them. "Ride up and tell McNelly to git ready to fight. The enemy's attackin' right away. Tell him to place his Rangers close to town on the west side, along the main trail, but not to show till he sees us. Then he kin make his charge. Got it?"

"*Si*, General," Mireles cried.

He sprang to his mustang's back. Low over the animal's body, he galloped full speed for Captain McNelly's camp.

"It'll take McNelly an hour to git down and in position," growled the Kid. He mounted the dun. "We got to delay Vance and his men till then, Big Foot."

Dan Worrell jumped awake, gun in his hand before he was on his feet.

Someone was just outside the shack where he slept, behind Purcell's big general store.

"Worrell!" He recognized the whispered voice. Unbarring the door, he leaped out to grasp the Rio Kid's hand.

"Bob!" Dan gasped. "What's up?"

"No time to explain," the Rio Kid said quickly. "Vance is attackin' wholesale. Rouse yore men and git inside the store. And make shore the front door's locked —"

"Here they come!" Worrell cried.

The beat of eight hundred hoofs rocked the earth. Sorreltop Vance, guns ready, came sweeping into Smithville, bravos and killers at his back.

The houses were dark. Few were awake at this hour of the night.

"C'mon," Worrell shouted, and he gave a war-whoop designed as a warning signal to the people of Smithville.

Vance and a big detachment split off, veering toward the store. Smaller groups headed for various homes.

"Git inside and bolt that front door, Worrell!" the Kid snapped.

Worrell was too good a fighting man to disobey. He rushed through and roused the guards in the kitchen. Purcell came bounding from his bedroom, his Sharps rifle in hand. Dan glimpsed Conchita's pale face as she looked from her room to see what was wrong.

Not a shot had been fired yet. The stunning attack had been quiet and direct as a striking rattler.

Worrell made the front door. To his surprise he found it unbolted, though it should have been locked for the night, with so much danger threatening. There was a glass window two-thirds of the way up the thick oaken panel. As Worrell got the big wooden bar into its guides, he glanced through the window. He saw dark figures throw themselves from their mounts and head for the store.

A dozen of them leaped onto the front porch. Worrell glimpsed Sorreltop Vance, in the midst of these. The rest, splitting, took the sides and hustled to the rear.

Already shots were coming from down the street and across the plaza as the fight began.

"Stand back or I'll fire," bawled Worrell, crashing his rifle barrel through the glass.

His answer was a hurried volley from the Colts of the approaching hombres. He heard the dull thud-thud of bullets in the thick oak panels, but it had been designed to stop slugs. He pulled his trigger. A Mexican outside shrieked and keeled over. Then Worrell ducked, knowing they would blast that window.

They did, thick and fast, an instant after he let go. . . .

Chapter XIX
Smithville Fights Back

Volleys of shots from the rear of the building blasted Worrell's eardrums. He heard the yells of fighting men as blood heated to the battle.

He jumped, keeping low. Slugs poured through the door opening. The gunnies began ramming it with their shoulders. To the right of the entrance was a window, for light and air. But it had a bar in it and was looped for guns. In Texas the Comanches and Apaches still raided towns when the moon was full, and Purcell had built his home for defense against them.

Worrell stuck his rifle through this opening. It was so arranged that he could angle his guns without standing directly in front of the opening itself.

He emptied his gun into the massed men around Vance as they strove to burst in the front door.

Sorreltop Vance uttered a cursing shriek.

Dan saw him jump away from the door, hopping on one foot.

"Fire!" bellowed Sorreltop, down on the step under the low-hanging roof. "Burn the skunks out!"

Then, Worrell hastily shoving cartridges into his rifle, gave a gasp of astonishment.

Sorreltop Vance suddenly flew up into the air, disappearing as though he had wings. Worrell glimpsed his kicking legs as the redhead vanished from sight.

Conchita set up a screaming that Dan Worrell could not ignore. He rushed back to join his sweetheart. A couple of Purcell's guards met him in the doorway between the store and the living quarters at the rear.

"What's wrong?" gasped Dan.

"The old man's hit," one of them yelled.

"Take the front. I'll git back with her."

He found his sweetheart collapsed over the prostrate body of her father. A bullet had found Purcell as he knelt at a loophole window, defending his home.

Lead thudded into the store walls, shrieked through the openings. The hail was answered by Purcell's handful of fighting men.

Dan Worrell knelt beside Purcell. The stocky pioneer storeman lay still, broad Irish face unmoving. His eyes were shut.

Worrell knew gun wounds. He hastily sought for the injury, found it in the head. A nasty furrow from a .45 bullet had sent Purcell low.

"Git some hot water quick, Conchita. Here, we'll put him on the bunk."

Worrell easily lifted the heavy storekeeper. Conchita pulled herself together, hurriedly heated water to dress her father's wound.

The blasting guns, the shrieks of hate and fear, dominated Smithville. The attack was on in full fury now.

There was no time for Worrell to attend Purcell. Every hand was needed to defend the store. He could smell the odor of burning wood. Red gleamed through the narrow window openings. Up front, the gunnies were still trying to get in.

Worrell grabbed his rifle and jumped toward a window to fight.

Up on the wide, flat roof of Purcell's General Store, the Rio Kid, gun in one hand, whispered hastily to his friend.

"Don't bust his neck yet, Big Foot. There's a murder charge against me in this town and I figger Vance kin help clear me of it."

"Don't worry," growled Wallace. "I'm holdin' him the way yuh do a snake."

Big Foot Wallace, lying flat on the porch roof over the steps, had scooped up Sorreltop Vance. The Rio Kid had braced Wallace's legs so the big fellow wouldn't slide off. Now they held prisoner the leader of the great array of killers attempting to down Smithville.

Shoving back, keeping low so they would not be seen from below, the two dragged the struggling, terrified Vance to the middle of the wide roof. A foot-high parapet, for Indian fighting, ran all around the building.

Wallace had Vance by the throat. He used just the right amount of pressure so the redhead could get some air yet could not cry out.

Sorreltop's cruel eyes bulged in fright. He realized that the Rio Kid had him. He waited for the death blow, but it didn't come. Instead, they rapidly tied him up with strips of his own shirt, thrust a bandanna gag into his mouth and left him lying in the center of the roof.

"See yuh later, Sorreltop," the Kid remarked. "We got business to tend to jest at present."

The odor of burning wood, the cries of wounded, curses of fighters, filled the air. Guns loaded, the two went to the edge of the roof. Leaning over the rail, they could look right down on a party of bravos who were piling dry brush against the store wall.

Then torches were brought up to light the blaze.

With scientific accuracy, Pryor and Big Foot began triggering their carbines. Those who could run did the best scrambling in their lives. But plenty of bodies stayed behind, motionless in the dirt.

Down below, the fight still raged. The store defenders succeeded in holding off the gunnies with the aid of Big Foot and the Rio Kid, up on the point of vantage of the roof.

The stiff battle waging around Purcell's drew more and more of the gunnies. The sudden disappearance of Sorreltop Vance worried them. His men had not seen him snatched aloft in the shadowy night, so quickly had it been accomplished. They could hear bravos calling for Vance. Most of the lieutenants had been wiped out by the Rio Kid and McNelly in Mexico during the Las Cuevas attack.

At other points smaller groups were at work, forcing into the homes of Smithville citizens. Guns blasted everywhere.

"Reckon I better git down and try to pull 'em out," the Rio Kid told Big Foot. "And it's time McNelly came up. Stick here and hold this red-haired lollopaloozer for me, Big Foot. See yuh in hell or sooner."

He ran to a corner of the roof. His whistle shrilled above the roar of battle, and the dun came galloping to the rear of Purcell's. Startled cries went up as the Rio Kid dropped from the low roof into his saddle. Spurs dug in and Colts blasting them, he rode hell-for-leather across the plaza.

"Ees ze Rio Keed!" shrieked a Mex. "After heem, men!"

The hot slugs of the Rio Kid tore through flesh and bone. Whooping like a madman, the Kid zigzagged over the plaza. Saber, with ears back and teeth bared, was making his fastest pace.

There were gunnies on the porches. The Kid's pistols sought them. He picked off one here, another there, as he rode west along the line of homes. A bunch of gunmen, eagerly following him on horseback, picked up recruits on the way.

He saw the jail door open, glimpsed the tall figure of Sheriff Dave Carr. The officer was bellowing, evidently ordering the attackers to desist as he came forth, guns in hand. But the Kid had no time to pause. His pursuers, at least forty of them, were spurring toward him. He glanced back over his shoulder, blue eyes shining with the excitement and joy of battle.

It was not far to the western screen of

brush. He knew that by this time McNelly should be charging in with his men.

Hot on the Kid's trail came the bunched gunnies, roaring and firing after him. The shriek of lead was in his ears as Pryor zigzagged at mad speed for the creek.

He hit the chaparral and passed on to the west trail out of Smithville. Directly ahead he saw the Rangers, McNelly sitting his saddle in the lead. They crossed the creek, two dozen of the best fighting men in the world. The Rio Kid whirled up, the dun rearing on his hind legs at the suddenness of the stop.

"Here they come, Cap'n!" the Kid cried. "S'pose yuh push back a little into the brush —"

McNelly snapped the order. The Rangers hurriedly drew to either side, up on the creek bank where the timber was thickest.

Hardly had they got out of sight when the van of the pursuers appeared, low over their horses, eyes shining with blood lust. They knew that the Rio Kid had made them tall trouble, and revenge loomed sweet.

The bunched horsemen whirled to the trap. Ranger guns blared into them, and half of them went down under McNelly's first volley. All his men were expert marksmen, cool and trained in a fight.

Screeches rose thick in the night air. The Rangers, with a war-whoop, charged out on the remaining gunnies. A few at the rear of the procession got turned and out of the crush. Scattering every way, they ignored the tearing thorns of the chaparral.

But the rest were caught in a horrible tangle of dead men and falling horses. Within seconds, McNelly was not taking prisoners, the entire bunch had succumbed, with hardly a damaging shot fired at the Rangers.

Leaving the dead and dying gunny bunch behind, McNelly and the Rio Kid skirted around the awful scene. The Kid sang out:

"Make it a circle, Cap'n. There's a hundred and twenty more in the town."

They burst out onto the village. Whooping and shooting, the Rangers under Captain McNelly charged the enemy. The bravos had believed McNelly to be miles away, in Rio Grande City. The sight of the victors of Las Cuevas appalled them.

Sorreltop Vance, their trusted boss, was not there to lead them. The gunnies afoot scrambled for their horses as the Rangers charged them. Each officer took on a dozen bravos, every shot with his Colt counting for a victim.

McNelly was in the thick of it, blasting

the foe with a browned-steel Colt.

The din and blare of firearms rang high over Smithville. The Rio Kid, on the fighting dun, rode swiftly up and down the line of homes. He shot into the running gunnies who were hastily deserting their prey as the alarmed yells of their mates reached their ears over the noise of the guns. They realized that now they were being opposed by Rangers. That was far different from attacking a helpless town.

Shifting Colts, Pryor swung at the end of the line of homes. He started back again, shooting and whooping it up. From Purcell's, he saw a rifle flashing off the roof, knew that Big Foot Wallace was enjoying himself up there. A dry grin touched his wide mouth.

"Nothin' Big Foot fancies so much as a good fight against odds," he chuckled, as he knocked a bravo off a porch.

The Rangers had circled the settlement. Everywhere it was possible to see one of them taking care of a bunch of the foe. Demoralized, half their number gone in the first flush of the fight, Vance's men began to look for escape. Horses were swung in retreat. But it seemed that the Rangers were everywhere. And whenever a gap was found, the Rio Kid came whirling up to close it.

As the gunnies locked for a death grip with McNelly's men, doors began opening. Citizens, armed with shotguns and Colts, issued forth to avenge the attack.

The crowd around the store had melted away into desperate individuals hunting for a way out of the trap. Dan Worrell came forth, leading three of Purcell's men, all who could now walk and shoot.

Bleeding from half a dozen bullet nicks, the Rio Kid reloaded his hot guns, and the bloody cleanup proceeded. No quarter was given or asked and both sides knew it. Individual conflicts raged. The Smithville folks were really piling into the fray. Participants went at one another, oblivious to the mass bloodshed all around them.

Over the plaza rolled a great cloud of powder smoke, mixed with choking dust from stamping feet and hoofs. Screeches of injured horses, curses of men, sharp bangs of revolvers, roar of shotguns that were useful in close work, mingled into a bedlam of horror.

Here and there a gunny managed to charge through and make the chaparral, escaping into the darkness. But the big gang mustered by Sorreltop Vance to crush Smithville was smashed forever. The Rangers, aided by the Rio Kid and the inhabitants of the settlement, wreaked their revenge for the thieving and brutal killings they had suffered at the hands of these rascals.

Even now the shooting was diminishing in volume. The few surviving gunnies were fighting across the bodies of dead horses and men. Ranger yells ripped raucous and fierce over the battlefield.

"That's about all," muttered the Rio Kid, blowing smoke from the barrel of his browned-steel Colt. "Reckon now I got time to go to work on Senor Vance!"

CHAPTER XX
WHO IS THE CHIEF?

His dun showed the effects of battle. Mustang hair filled Saber's mouth, for he had done more than his share of the fighting. Biting and lunging at the horses of the Kid's opponents, Saber had rushed the other animals off balance, ruining the aim of their riders.

The Rio Kid roweled the dun for Purcell's store. The fires which the desperadoes had tried to start were only smoking piles. Now that the fighting was about over, Worrell was directing the men as they threw pails of water over the burnt, hot areas.

Crowds of Smithville people rolled over the plaza. The killers who had sought to finish them were being finished themselves.

"Hi, Bob," sang out Dan, as the Rio Kid dismounted in front of the store. "Yuh shore saved the day, the Rangers and you!"

The Rio Kid grinned. Slouching with weight on one leg, handsome face stained with dirt and powder dust, he rolled a quirly.

"I heard yore girl yellin'," Pryor said. "She hurt?"

"Nope, but her dad took one in the head."

"Is he bad hit?"

"Not so bad he won't git well. It's a nasty, deep crease, but I don't reckon he'll be discommoded long."

"Hey, there, Rio Kid!" a voice hailed from the roof parapet. "Git me a ladder, will yuh? I'm 'fraid to jump."

Big Foot Wallace, who had performed prodigious feats of slaughter with his rifle that night from his eyrie, peeked over the edge at Bob Pryor.

"I feel like a vulture, a-settin' up here."

"Pass down that red-haired snake first," the Kid ordered.

Wallace went back out of sight and returned, dragging Sorreltop Vance along with him. He lowered the hog-tied prisoner to Worrell and the Rio Kid. They let Vance fall to the dirt, while they gave the giant frontiersman a hand in reaching the ground. Big Foot was heavy and did not want to land on something in the shadows and perhaps wrench a muscle. He was getting on in years.

"Fetch Vance along, will yuh?" Pryor said. "C'mon, we'll see kin we find Old Casuse.

There's got to be some talkin' done and pronto."

Sorreltop Vance was fully awake. His greenish eyes rolled with fear in his ugly red head. The gag was tightly strapped across the prickly beard and mouth.

"He's shore a nasty lookin' devil," remarked Big Foot. "Why, I'd shoot him on sight, Kid, jest to be shore."

The battle was over. Smithville had won. Yet the Rio Kid knew that there still remained the task of unmasking the chief, Vance's director in the Black Heart murders, the unscrupulous fiend who had tried to win the entire county for himself.

Old Casuse had fought with the Rangers through the scrap. Now he was lounging with his broad back to a doorstep, cigarette curling smoke up around his huge handlebar mustache. His seamed face wrinkled to a grin as he recognized his friend, the Rio Kid.

"Aha, Keed, you get eenuff fight tonight?" the Mexican Ranger cried.

As yet the citizens had not spotted the lithe Rio Kid. Dressed much like one of the Rangers, he had been mistaken for a McNelly man.

"Enough for the time bein'," the Rio Kid laughed. "But we still got a little job to do, Casuse. Where's yore old paint horse?"

223

"Oh, right over zere," the Mexican answered. "He tire', Keed. No like to fight. Rather sleep."

Celestino Mireles, Big Foot Wallace, Bill Callicott of the Rangers, Lieutenant Robinson, Sergeants Orell and Hall, and the rank-and-file of McNelly's handful of heroes, came gathering around the group.

Citizens joined them, many carrying lanterns and flaring torches which cast a glow over the actors in the scene that ensued.

At the Rio Kid's bidding, Casuse fetched the paint horse. The animal's head bobbed sleepily as he slowly followed his master to the tall oak at one corner of the plaza.

Sorreltop Vance was stood up under a long limb that stuck straight out from the trunk.

Pryor pulled off the bandanna gag, slashed the rope binding the killer's ankles. He noosed a lariat and dropped it around Sorreltop's scrawny neck, tossing the other end over the limb above.

"Put him aboard, Big Foot," the Kid growled.

Wallace lifted the big leader of the gunnies to the paint horse's saddle. Vance's ugly face contorted with terror.

"Don't — don't —" he gasped.

"Go on, make him talk, Casuse," commanded the Kid. "He's got plenty to tell."

"Hey!" an excited Mexican-American cried. "Zat hombre ees ze Rio Keed, who keeled Espinosa. He ees pal of Vance —"

A tall figure shouldered through the crowd. Sheriff Dave Carr shouted:

"You come with me, Rio Kid! Yuh're wanted for murder! This is my town, and I mean to enforce the law in it. Quit torturin' that pris'ner!"

Captain McNelly barked through. A quick command sent his Texas Rangers into a circle, facing outward around the oak tree. Big Foot Wallace and Dan Worrell helped block off the sheriff and citizens against any move against Bob Pryor.

Wallace shoved Carr in the face, driving him off.

"Keep shut, Sheriff. Listen to a real law officer," he growled.

"Stand back, folks," McNelly told them quietly but firmly. "You'll have to give the Kid a chance!"

Bob Pryor nudged old Casuse. The Mexican seized hold of the lariat end and yanked Sorreltop Vance up off the saddle. The paint horse was dozing with head down.

"Talk, Vance!" the Kid cried. "Tell 'em who's yore boss. Who planned them Black Heart murders?"

Sorreltop gritted his teeth. Casuse let him down when he began to gasp.

"Folks," Bob Pryor declared, so all could hear, "yuh've made a big mistake 'bout me. I told yuh I was planted. Some snake put that black cowhide and the knife in my pack while my saddle hung on the livery stable fence. Vance'll tell yuh the reason.

"Under yore town is an old Spanish mine that the Jesuits run. When they was expelled from Mexico, they hid their workin's, covered 'em with stones, dirt and sod, so's they couldn't be found. They swore the Indians to keep the secrets. There're galleries of a gold mine beneath Smithville. Whoever owns the land has title to the metal. It's worth a big fortune, and Vance and his pals were after it.

"They worked with Gonzales and the rustlers from Las Cuevas. In return for killers to help him, the chief of all this murderous business meant to give the Mexes a clear road through to the Rio Grande for their stolen beeves. As for them Black Heart murders, they were done thataway to scare yuh, force as many folks as possible to leave and give up their holdin's, sell 'em for a song or desert 'em altogether. I got a bit too close to the truth, so Vance's chief framed me on that Espinosa killin'."

Sorreltop Vance, breathing hard, stared with incredulous, bulging eyes at the Rio Kid.

"They was not on'y clearin' the Texas side," drawled on Pryor. "They got a bunch of titles across the river, too, so's to get the whole huge Spanish grant, folks. George Purcell owns 'bout a quarter of yore settlement here. He'd been dead long ago on'y he had luck and hired bodyguards to watch day and night. The others who died were all possible heirs of the Spanish grant or likely to cause trouble 'bout the claim."

Again the Kid signaled Casuse, and Sorreltop Vance was hoisted out of the paint horse's saddle. When he landed, Vance fought for air and then gasped, realizing the secret was public.

"He's tellin' — the truth, folks — I — the chief — wanted — the mine —"

A growl of fury started in the throats of the crowd. They surged forward, but the Rangers stood between them and their prey.

"C'mon, who's this chief yuh mention?" demanded Bob Pryor quickly. "Is the hombre here who planted that murder on me?"

"There — there — he is — damn him. He got me into — this —"

Sorreltop Vance couldn't point, for his hands were tied behind his back. He nodded toward someone in the crowd. The Rio Kid turned to see who it was.

As the Kid shifted, a bullet hit his Stetson brim and wounded a spectator in the upper arm. The crack of the shot echoed across the plaza. The cursing of the wounded citizen was punctuated by the scream of a woman.

"There he goes! Stop him!"

Sheriff Dave Carr had made the hasty shot at the Rio Kid and Sorreltop Vance. He was edging to the outskirts of the crowd while Pryor and Casuse worked on the red-haired prisoner.

Carr streaked for the adobe-walled jail, his headquarters. He had a room in back where he slept and cooked his meals. They saw the tall, burly figure jump inside, heard the slam of the door, the bang of the dropping bolt.

A gasp went up from the citizens. For a moment they stood, unable to believe that the man they had elected to protect them was a murderous conniver, who had cold-bloodedly killed in order to clear the old Spanish title for himself.

"It's Carr," croaked Sorreltop Vance. He was taking vicious delight in dragging his director into the same mess he was in.

The sheriff's fight clinched his guilt. With

a roar of fury the citizens of Smithville grasped their weapons and started for the jail. Rangers were bowled out of the way. In the din, orders could not be heard. McNelly quickly rallied his men, meaning to keep the crowd from a lynching bee.

The jail was dark. A gun stuck through the narrow window in front, crashed a bullet into the crowd, killing a citizen in the lead. Then a fusillade from many guns roared back, spattering on the thick adobe wall.

No more shots came from inside. McNelly, calling to his men, led them toward the jail. He would take charge and keep the crowd in order.

The Rio Kid was one of the first to reach the front door. It was barred and built of tremendously thick and hard oak panels.

"Git some crowbars and a fence rail," someone yelled. "Smash her in, boys!"

CHAPTER XXI
END OF
THE KILLER TRAIL

Noiselessly, the Rio Kid darted around to the sides, hunting a way in. The windows were all barred, most of them too narrow to admit even a slim man. The back door was as thick and strongly bolted as the front.

The man who had trapped himself inside could hardly hope to escape for long. Dozens of willing hands had hauled a tree trunk from a nearby woodpile. The thick, heavy battering-ram pounded rhythmically against the street door. Hollowly the jail echoed the thuds.

But the door had been made to withstand battering. Though they could not hope to smash it down, they did manage to make it give an inch at the bottom. Then they were able to get their steel crowbars into the crack and exert leverage. The door creaked and groaned, as half a dozen men put their weight on the bars.

The Rangers stood aside, allowing the

crowd to get the door open for them.

When the door fell off its hinges, McNelly and his men sprang in from both sides, cutting off the crowd, blocking them with rifle barrels.

"I'll arrest the sheriff, gents," the captain called. "I'll defend him, too. Stand back."

The Rio Kid and McNelly, guns drawn, hastily ran through the jail. There was a cell to the right, the sheriff's table and office to the left.

"Strike a match," McNelly ordered.

Pryor did so. Outside, the crowd growled its disappointment. But they would not monkey with the Ranger captain's business.

A candle stood on Carr's table. Pryor lit the blackened wick, picked it up. They started into the rear of the place, carefully, McNelly calling out:

"Come out with your hands up, Carr! You're under arrest."

Neither bullets nor curses answered. The back room, with its bunk and blankets, cookstove and food on shelves, was as empty as the front.

McNelly stared around, and so did the Kid.

"Now where the hell did he go!" muttered Pryor.

He stooped, gun in hand, to peek under

the bunk. The candle cast a shallow beam. The sheriff wasn't hiding under the bed, and there was no place else —

Suddenly the Kid gave a cry of surprise. He got down on his hands and knees and crawled under the bunk.

"Hey, Captain," he said, "there's a hole in the ground under here! It must lead into the mine. So that's how come he found it! I reckon he either had a little cave-in or else noticed how hollow the earth sounded."

"Well, let's get in and trail him, quick," McNelly cried.

A rough ladder, made of wooden strips nailed across two poles, descended to the mine.

The Rio Kid and the captain dashed outside. McNelly hastily began calling orders to his men. Torches were being fetched in. Half a dozen Rangers, led by McNelly, were preparing to descend the ladder and chase the fleeing arch-killer, Sheriff Dave Carr.

"He's got a right good start," thought Pryor, as he fought a way through the crowd of Smithville citizens. "Must be three ways into the mine. One through the jail. One northeast, where Vance and his men come in when they bumped into me down there —"

He was running full-tilt for Saber, whistling to the dun.

Cautiously the Kid pushed through the chaparral along the west bank of the creek.

Suddenly, as he paused to listen, he heard the sound of something moving in the water. He was close upon the spot where the hidden canal into the Spanish mine emerged under the opposite bank. That third exit was nearest the Mexico trail. Pryor had figured that Carr would try to reach the Rio and escape into the wilds of the Mexican chaparral. Only the Kid's swift analysis, his mad gallop here on Saber, had cut off Carr's dash.

Against the blackness of the other bank he saw a paler patch that he knew was Dave Carr's face. The sheriff had made good his crawl through the narrow underground waterways. Now he turned to look around and make certain he was clear of pursuers.

"Carr!" Pryor called, voice sharp as an arrowhead. "Throw down yore gun and stand!"

Instantly the killer snarled his hatred. He shot at the direction of the Kid's voice. But he aimed too high, counting on the probability that the Rio Kid would be erect. But Pryor was lying flat, and the slug whistled an inch over his head. The sheriff started running down the rough creek bed. The Kid snaked out to the bank and let go with his Colt.

Once again Carr swung, to shoot at the flash of the Rio kid's pistol. The bullet from the murderous traitor, Sheriff Dave Carr, zipped into the mud bank. A second time Pryor fired. But even as he shot, he saw the arch-enemy stumble, falling face forward into the water.

The Kid's first slug had hit a vital spot. Carr's final bullet had come from a dying man's gun, the mere instinctive reaction of a killer.

Bob Pryor stepped into the creek, waded toward the spot where he had seen Carr go down. He found the sheriff lying half submerged on his side. The tawny water was stained with a darker fluid.

The Rio Kid pouched his Colt, seized the dead man by the arm, managed to shoulder him. Bent over, he staggered to the bank and whistled to Saber. The dun came pushing through the brush.

The Kid threw the body over the saddle and mounted behind.

A short while later he rode into Smithville plaza, and dumped the corpse at Captain McNelly's feet. The Ranger captain, called by his men, climbed up from the mine and emerged from the jail.

Worn out, the Rio Kid left the details to the Texas Rangers. Dan Worrell hurried up, seized the Kid's hand, pumped it.

"Yuh shore saved us all," he cried. "Anything I kin do, Bob, let me know. I own some land in town here and it'll shore be worth plenty. I reckon I kin marry Conchita and we kin buy us any kind of spread now. How 'bout some food?"

"A good idee," smiled Pryor. "And a drink wouldn't hurt either, Worrell."

Mireles and Big Foot Wallace hustled up and joined the two men as they started for Purcell's.

Passing the tall oak at the corner of the plaza, the Rio Kid frowned, stopped short with a curse. From the limb dangled a limp figure. Pryor didn't need to go closer to see that Sorreltop Vance had paid the killer's price.

He left the others and found Old Casuse taking a nap with his back to a house, his paint horse standing at his side. He nudged the Mexican awake.

"Hey, Casuse," he growled. "What happened?"

"Huh, what you mean, Keed?"

"How come yuh hung Vance? The law should've tended to that."

Casuse looked up into the Kid's face, and winked solemnly.

"Ev'rybody run 'way, go eenside, Rio Keed. Old Casuse's foot sleeped!"

"Yore foot slipped, huh!"

The Rio Kid shrugged. There was nothing to be done about it now that Vance was dead. He knew it had only pushed forward Vance's execution date, anyhow. It was a rough land and a harsh time, and Casuse had suffered much at the hands of the thieves from Mexico.

The Kid stalked back to his pals. They all went over to the Purcells' and entered the lighted kitchen. In a bedroom, Conchita was sitting beside her father. She tiptoed out and shut the door. Then she kissed Worrell, who hugged her close.

"How is he?" Dan asked softly.

"Better," she replied. "He's asleep, and he ought to be all right in a week or so, Dan. You boys do look hungry. Wash up and I'll have something for you in a jiffy."

With drinks and food in them, the fighters felt better. Sleep tugged at the eyelids of the Rio Kid.

He rolled up in his blankets in Worrell's shack behind the store. Big Foot always slept on the floor if he could. He was so used to the earth that he felt uncomfortable in beds that were invariably too short for the giant frontiersman.

The sun was high and yellow when the Rio Kid rose the next day, buckled on his guns and belt, and washed up at the pump. After Conchita gave him food, he strolled across the plaza.

The Rangers were in camp there, and McNelly was talking with a handsome gentleman of hale and hearty middle age.

"Meet the Rio Kid," McNelly said. "Pryor, this is Cap'n Richard King, owner of Santa Gertrudis Ranch, one of the biggest spreads in Texas."

Pryor shook hands with the bluff, good-natured King. "The Kid gave us a big hand in Mexico," McNelly went on.

Captain King was deeply interested. He smiled at Bob Pryor, taking in the lithe figure of the reckless young fellow.

"Cap'n McNelly sent over a bunch of my cows that the thieves stole," King told the Kid. "They're the first steers I've got back since they began operatin'. I'll have to pin gold medals on 'em! Foolin' aside, though, I'm shore obliged to you for breaking up that gang. They took a big toll from me. I rode over here to thank Cap'n McNelly and you boys for all you've done and to tell you you're always welcome at the ranch. That attack on Mexico with thirty men is one of the bravest deeds I ever heard tell of."

The Rio Kid wasn't much for taking praise. He knew in his innermost heart that he rode the Frontier because he enjoyed it. Any other life that did not offer its dangers would not appeal to him.

A shrill whinny came from the corral near Purcell's. The Kid sniffed the aromatic scent of the chaparral, wafted to him on the warming breeze. Butterflies hovered over the flowers of the mesquite, and far to the west a smoke column showed in the azure sky.

Taking his leave of McNelly and Captain Richard King, he hustled over to get the dun, his pet and companion in so many adventures and perils.

Mireles was snoozing in the sun outside the store. Big Foot Wallace was packing up, making ready to return to his job of carrying U.S. mail across six hundred miles of Apache-infested wilderness between San Antonio and El Paso. Now that the fun was over, Big Foot's face was sad. He was thinking about the Lipan's moccasins, never to be his in this life.

Dan Worrell stepped to the kitchen door, sang out to his friend, the Rio Kid.

"C'mon in, Bob. Wanta talk to yuh 'bout

yore settlin' down here with us. I'll stake yuh to a plot of ground. I shore hope yuh'll let me do so and —"

Mireles woke up, looking anxious. He, too, had grown to love the wandering life they led, and he feared that an anchor would mean the end.

The Rio Kid smiled as he shook Dan Worrell's hand.

"Wish yuh luck, Dan. Yuh got a beautiful girl and yuh're as good as rich. But, me, I don't like houses. We're the kind that always gotta be ridin'. Reckon we'll go a way with Big Foot here, if he kin stand it."

"Shore kin," Wallace boomed.

Conchita heard them, came to beg them to stay. But the three were ready to go. They said farewell to their friends in Smithville. The Kid shook hands with Captain Mc-Nelly. He did not know it would be his last glimpse of this greatest of Rangers. McNelly could scarcely hold himself up except in the excitement of battle.

The Texas sun beat down on the three intrepid comrades as they rode out of the valley, headed westward into the wilderness. There the Rio Kid would continue to ride, hunting for the dangers he loved.

The employees of Thorndike Press hope you have enjoyed this Large Print book. All our Thorndike and Wheeler Large Print titles are designed for easy reading, and all our books are made to last. Other Thorndike Press Large Print books are available at your library, through selected bookstores, or directly from us.

For information about titles, please call:
(800) 223-1244

or visit our Web site at:
http://gale.cengage.com/thorndike

To share your comments, please write:
Publisher
Thorndike Press
295 Kennedy Memorial Drive
Waterville, ME 04901